I0659187

A FRIEND IN NEED

THE 72 DEMONS
BOOK TWO

JAMES E WISHER

SAND HILL PUBLISHING

Copyright © 2024 by James Wisher

All rights reserved.

No part of this book may be reproduced in any form or by any electronic or mechanical means, including information storage and retrieval systems, without written permission from the author, except for the use of brief quotations in a book review.

Edited by: Janie Linn Dullard

Cover art by: Stone Tower Studio

ISBN: 978-1-68520-070-1

31620241.0

CHAPTER ONE

C arter Monk had made many poor decisions in his life, but coming to Milden Station had to be right at the top of the list. As the hub for all trade in this sector of the outback, it was inevitable that his search for the demon prison would bring him here. When his brother's supply caravan arrived at his base camp two days ago bearing a note saying that the information he needed to complete his mission could be found here, Carter had to check it out.

He arrived a couple hours before sunset and started chatting with the locals. None of them had a clue, either about the note or anything resembling the demon prison. Then the sun set and everything went completely to hell.

Now Carter found himself sprinting through the dark down Milden Station's solitary road.

He glanced over his shoulder. A shadow flitted through the moonlight, passing between a pair of tin shacks before disappearing again.

It seemed whoever's punch bowl he'd pissed in was still

1

after him. As a member of the Circle of Sorcery, he had considerable skill in magical combat and an individual shadow was no match for him. The problem was, Carter had already destroyed three shadows and seriously doubted the one he just saw was the only one left. The bloody things just kept coming. Whoever summoned them was either exceptionally powerful or had been building up his or her—Carter really had no idea who he was dealing with—forces for some time. Before he could make up his mind which was the least-bad prospect, a shadow appeared right in front of him.

An instinctive blast of divine energy blew it to wisps of black flame.

That had been too close. He wiped sweat from his brow. Despite the sun having set an hour ago, the cursed heat lingered.

"Gah!" He twisted away from a stabbing pain in his back and staggered a step.

A shadow had snuck up behind him and the blow had drained a chunk of his strength.

A burst of divine energy exploded out in all directions, blowing the shadow away and leaving Carter even weaker. He needed to get the hell out of the station and back to his basecamp. Easier said than done considering his dune buggy and, more importantly, the supplies he needed were on the opposite end of town.

He also seriously doubted the shadows would just let him leave in peace. The first hint of a backlash headache was building and that boded ill for his long-term prospects.

His only small comfort came from the fact that he'd convinced Justine, his research assistant, to stay behind in camp. If Carter had had to protect her as well as himself, he'd be dead already.

Limping along as quickly as his limited strength would allow, he finally reached the edge of the station. A simple bar gate attached to a shack controlled access to the town. The guard who was supposed to be on night watch lay flat and limp on the ground beside it. A quick glance through the ether confirmed that his life force was still strong. Thank heaven for small favors.

In front of the gate six shadows had gathered, all of them bigger and more solid-looking than any he'd destroyed so far.

A black disk appeared in the middle of them and a shape oozed up out of it. The shape grew and became decidedly feminine in form. Finally, the blackness slid back into the disk and vanished, leaving a stunning brunette behind. He guessed her age around midtwenties. Silky black hair hung down to the middle of her back. Bloodred lips that looked even darker given her pale skin turned up in a smile when she looked at him. Normally that expression on a woman this beautiful would fill him with joy. When it was combined with her glowing red eyes, the effect was decidedly colder.

The black dress she wore did little to hide her curves. It was slit up to her hip on both sides and down the front to her belly button. How there was enough material to restrain her massive breasts was a mystery he'd ordinarily be delighted to explore.

Unfortunately, he was fairly certain she was the architect of his current predicament. He also had serious doubts about her humanity.

He spun only to find six more of the denser shadows closing in from behind. You've really stepped in it this time, Carter. Assuming he survived, the boss would never let him hear the end of it.

Fighting wasn't going to serve him now, so Carter raised his hands to the side and smiled. "Good evening. Fancy meeting a pretty lady like you in a place like this."

Not one of his better lines, but it had sounded sincere, at least to his ears.

"Good evening?" she said. From her accent he guessed she was French. What the hell was a French shadowmancer doing here of all places? "I think not. Nothing good ever comes from strangers visiting my station uninvited and asking questions best left unasked."

"Perhaps there's been a misunderstanding. I received a note yesterday inviting me here. I never would've come otherwise."

Her frown of displeasure didn't reduce her beauty in the slightest. "Who sent it?"

Carter shook his head and very slowly reached into the front pocket of his cargo shorts. He pulled the note out and offered it to her.

A tentacle of ether plucked it out of his hand and pulled it to her. She unfolded the note and read it. The process didn't take long as there were only two paragraphs and a stylized X for a signature.

She flicked the note away and it quickly crumbled to dust. "Someone, it seems, wants you dead."

"That surprises me less than it would most people. Look, I don't know who you are and I don't care about your business. How about we just go our separate ways? I promise never to come back."

"There's a part of me that's tempted to do just that if only to spite whoever had the audacity to think they could use me as their personal executioner." Carter's hopes rose just a fraction only to be dashed a moment later. "Unfortunately, I can't imagine a light caster like yourself simply forgetting what you've seen. Despite your best intentions, I fear you would eventually return with a larger force. Given the time and energy I've invested here, I can't risk it."

Carter gathered divine energy around his hands. As he did, the pounding in his head grew worse.

He might get off two blasts if he was lucky.

An explosion of darkness shot up all around him.

His light magic shield held for a few seconds.

When it broke, a moment of blinding pain was followed by nothingness.

CHAPTER TWO

Daisuke Kugo lay snuggled up under the covers of his bed, smiling at the ceiling. A little bit of light leaked in around the heavy drapes covering his window. He had no idea what time it was and couldn't have cared less if he did. Four days of rest had done wonders to restore his strength after the mission in Japan.

Not that he'd rested the whole time. He looked down at the top of Helena's head where she slept tucked up beside him, her blond hair spread out on the pillow like a halo. She'd been a most agreeable companion these past few days. Being with her took his mind almost completely off his family.

Which was a good thing given the mood he'd been in after dealing with the Kugo clan on a fairly steady basis. Seeing his mother and brother had been nice enough. Daisuke even enjoyed fighting beside Natsumi, though when they weren't fighting, she did get on his nerves. The rest of the clan, Yoshikazu in particular, had done nothing but make his job harder.

Well, the hell with them. They were half a world away and not his problem.

He was just about to roll over and put his arm around Helena when his phone rang. Half a second later Helena's joined in. Four days was a pretty good rest for him. But he suspected it was time to get back to work.

He grabbed his phone on the second ring. "Yeah, boss?"

"I need you in my office, ASAP. I assume Helena's with you. Bring her."

She sounded as worked up as Daisuke had ever heard. "What's up?"

"I'll tell you in person. Get here, now." The line went dead.

Daisuke shook his head and turned to find Helena awake and leaning on one elbow, staring at him. Talk about a beautiful sight. "That sounded bad."

"Yup. Much as I'd like to, I fear we'd best not dillydally."

They got out of bed and hunted for clothes that had been scattered around the bedroom the night before. Daisuke finished first, pocketing his phone and a rectangle of metal the size of a playing card that could transform into a large trunk. He'd never bothered to unpack after getting home from Japan and now he suspected that would turn out to be a good decision.

"Ruq." His imp familiar shimmered into view a few feet away. Two feet tall with red, scaly skin and a scorpion tail, Ruq had been with Daisuke for a few years, ever since he found the imp locked in a cage and left to die by the cult of Abaddon. He usually took the form of a rat, but for some reason decided to go with his demon shape today.

"Have you completed your fornications, Master?"

"For the moment. Call in a to-go order for breakfast at the bakery. We'll eat on our way to the shop."

While Helena finished dressing and Ruq saw to breakfast, Daisuke slipped into the bathroom to wash his face and brush his teeth.

Fifteen minutes after the boss's call, they were outside and on their way down the busy streets of Zurich. It was warm enough this morning that his usual black t-shirt felt just right. Helena looked stunning in a white blouse and jeans just tight enough to show off her well-toned legs. Of course, Helena would look stunning in a burlap sack, so there was that.

"What do you suppose happened to get her so worked up?" Helena asked.

"The archangels know. Maybe she got a line on another demon prison. Though she wasn't this anxious when the last one came to light."

They reached Stein's Bakery ten minutes after leaving his apartment. The glass front was filled with all manner of breads and cakes. The scent wafting out the open front door was what Daisuke imagined Heaven smelled like. It was a dream for a sugar junkie like him.

"Sure you don't want anything?" he asked.

"I usually skip breakfast and even if I didn't, I certainly wouldn't eat what you do."

"You're as bad as the boss. I'll just be a sec."

He ducked inside and went right up to the empty counter. Other than a pair of old ladies perusing the baguettes, he was the only customer. One good thing about getting here around midmorning; he avoided the breakfast rush. A middle-aged bald man covered in flour emerged from the kitchen with a large brown bag and hurried up to the counter.

"Morning, Daisuke. Here's your order. I added it to your account."

"Thanks, Mr. Stein." Daisuke put his debit card on the counter. "We'd better settle up. Looks like I'll be heading out of town for work again."

"You'll run yourself ragged, my boy." Mr. Stein swiped the card then handed it back with a receipt that Daisuke signed. "Have a good trip."

"Thanks. Say hi to Mrs. Stein for me." He waved and strode out the front door.

Helena fell in beside him and they headed for headquarters. Daisuke held out a doughnut that vanished into thin air then got one for himself. By the time they reached Arcane Books and Trinkets, the Circle of Sorcery's front business, he and Ruq had polished off a dozen doughnuts.

Recharged and ready to go, Daisuke unlocked the back door and made the short walk to the boss's office. He knocked and she immediately said, "Come in."

As soon as he opened the door smoke came billowing out. Through the haze he spotted the boss pacing and sucking on a half-burned-up cigarette. Her faintly glowing yellow eyes looked a bit brighter than usual today. Ten still-smoldering butts littered the ash tray on her desk. The boss wore a gray suit that blended perfectly with the smoke and made it look like she was fading in and out of view.

A wave of his hand summoned a gust of wind to blow the rest of the smoke out. As soon as Helena closed the door behind them the boss skewered him with her glowing yellow eyes. "Where have you been? I said to get here immediately."

"Immediately would've meant naked and hungry,"

Daisuke said. "I made an executive decision to get dressed and order takeout. What's got you so riled up, boss?"

She stabbed out her cigarette, pointed at the empty chairs in front of her desk, and sat in her own. When Daisuke and Helena had settled in she said, "Two days ago Carter Monk contacted me. He was on a mission in Australia. An unknown party sent him a message and asked to meet at one of the outback stations. The note he received said that whoever sent it had information that was vital to Carter's mission. Carter smelled a rat, but didn't dare ignore whoever sent the note. He missed his last contact window and the next one is coming up in an hour. If he misses that one…"

Daisuke had been listening to the boss, but his gaze was locked on Helena. The usually unflappable blond beauty was trembling and her eyebrows had drawn down, narrowing her eyes. It seemed both the ladies in his life were reacting stronger than usual to this mission.

"I got it, boss. If he misses this one, he'll be officially deemed missing and you'll need to decide if you want to send a rescue party. Since Helena and I are here, I'm guessing the answer to that question will be yes."

"You're absolutely correct," the boss said. "And not just because Carter is one of our most experienced field agents. I believe the person that contacted him is an old friend of mine that I thought vanished a decade ago."

Daisuke ran a hand through his hair, glanced at Helena, who seemed to have herself back under control, and said, "We've got an hour before we know for sure. Why don't you tell us everything from the beginning?"

"Good idea." The boss reached for a cigarette, put it in her mouth, took it out, and shook her head. "It started a month ago when I spotted a symbol in some Aboriginal art that was a perfect match for one of the demon symbols. It could've been a coincidence, but I don't believe in them. I sent Carter to get to the bottom of it. He's an Australian citizen, which meant he was free to enter the country openly. He found a scholar at Sydney University that was studying Aboriginal symbology and convinced her to team up with him."

Helena smiled. "Carter always had a way with the ladies."

That statement raised even more questions in Daisuke's mind, not that any of them were pertinent to the current discussion.

"Carter and the student, Justine, headed into the outback to examine the paintings that featured the demon mark. His reports were regular, short, and boring. He found the site but there was nothing magical, much less demonic, present. There were some other sites of interest not too far off and he hoped to speak with a local shaman. Two days ago he contacted me about the note." She picked up a paper and handed it to Daisuke. "I printed that from a picture he took of the original."

Helena scooted closer to read over his shoulder. Not that there was much to read. It said, "I have some information that's vital to your mission. Meet me at Milden Station tomorrow. I will only discuss the details in person." It was signed with a fancy capital X.

"Not much to go on, boss. I assume he went because whoever sent the note knew enough about his business to find him out in the middle of nowhere."

"Correct. That X is how my friend Xerxes always signed his name. I haven't seen or talked to him in ten years. The last time we spoke he said he was on the trail of a book that wasn't supposed to exist. It's the companion text to the Book of Wisdom. Supposedly started by Solomon the Wise and finished by his eldest son."

"Okay, I'll bite," Daisuke said. "What's so amazing about this book besides the authors?"

"It's supposed to contain a spell that, when used in conjunction with the Book of Wisdom, will allow the caster to locate any of the prisons or seals no matter where in the world they are."

Daisuke whistled. "Wow. Yeah, I can see how that would be useful. Did Xerxes know you had the Book of Wisdom?"

"Yes. He helped me find it. That was before I founded the Circle of Sorcery. I wanted him to help me recruit members, but he said finding the second book was more important. If he's finally found it, that could be the advantage we need to beat the Blood of Solomon to all the prisons."

"Any chance he's gone bad and led Carter into a trap?" Helena asked.

"None. There's no more trustworthy being on the planet than Xerxes."

"Okay," Daisuke said. "So I guess the plan is for Helena and I to go to Australia, figure out what happened to Carter, and see if we can track down your friend. If we can find the second book and a demon prison, that'll be a bonus."

"That's the mission," the boss said. "Assuming Carter doesn't call in the next fifteen minutes."

That seemed pretty unlikely, but Daisuke didn't want to say anything given how anxious both ladies were.

"Two more questions," he said. "Unlike Carter, Helena and I aren't citizens and Australia is a closed nation. How are we supposed to get there? I can't shadow walk somewhere I've never been."

"They may not let noncitizens enter, but they do allow

overflights. You'll have to parachute in then shadow walk home."

Helena swallowed audibly. "I've never parachuted before."

"We're wizards," Daisuke said. "That's what flying spells are for."

"I don't know that spell." Helena choked out each word.

Daisuke grinned. "I do, and you know I like to share."

"What's your other question?" the boss asked.

"Right, assuming the demon mark is actually what it looks like, who are we dealing with?"

"Konoth, a greater demon in service to Baphomet, Lord of the Corrupt Earth."

CHAPTER THREE

They ended up waiting half an hour to be sure, but just as Daisuke feared, Carter's call never came. Now he was standing outside an apartment building ten blocks from the shop, waiting for Helena to gather her gear. He didn't know if she had an extra-dimensional trunk like his, but he hoped either she did or she packed light.

At least there were no people around at the moment. It was midday and they were all probably at work, blissfully unaware of all the potential ways the world might come to an end. Taking care of that was wizards' work and it had been since they revealed their existence while saving humanity from complete extinction in a nuclear holocaust. Though well before his time, Daisuke was fairly sure no one ever said thank you.

"Are you intentionally trying to avoid thinking about the mission?" Ruq asked. Even though Daisuke was used to it, hearing the imp's voice coming from thin air still seemed strange.

"There's nothing to think about. I have lots of questions and no one who can answer them."

"Your boss might have answered some of them. You didn't press very hard before accepting the mission."

"You mean about her mysterious friend, Xerxes? It's none of my business. Not that I plan to trust him just because she says he's totally trustworthy. Someone set Carter up and Xerxes is the most likely candidate. As for the rest of my questions, if the boss knew any more intel, she'd have shared it. Justine should have more details."

"Assuming she doesn't die of a heart attack when a pair of wizards drop out of the sky."

"If she went alone into the outback with Carter, she's got to be made of sterner stuff than that."

Helena emerged from the apartment building with a mercifully small pack on her back. "I'm good to go. There's a cab on the way to take us to the airport."

"About that. You can't jump out of a regular plane. What are we flying in?"

Helena shrugged. "Beats me, but I assume whatever the boss set up will work. She'd never make such an amateur mistake."

She was right about that. Logistics were the boss's specialty.

A black and white taxi pulled up and they piled in. As soon as the door closed, they were zooming toward the airport. It was on the opposite side of Zurich, so they had a good half-hour drive. The cabby wasn't the talkative sort, thank the universe, and he and Helena couldn't exactly discuss the mission in public. Not that there was much to discuss until they were on site and had more information.

The cab pulled up outside a warehouse attached to the

runway at the very edge of the airport. Several windows were broken and the big double doors were wide open. It wasn't the sort of place that filled Daisuke with confidence. Then he reminded himself again that the boss's specialty was logistics and that surely there was a plane inside that was flightworthy.

"You two sure this is where you want to be?" the cabby asked in a disbelieving tone that was totally understandable.

"It's the right address." Helena handed him a folded-up bill and said, "Keep the change."

They got out and the cabby took off like he was afraid he'd end up getting mugged if he stuck around a moment longer than necessary. That seemed like a bit of an overreaction. The area wasn't that bad aside from the warehouse itself.

There was no fence or security or anything, so they hiked down a rough, paved road to the front of the warehouse. There was nothing magical here and when he checked, Daisuke sensed only one life form. Since the doors were open he saw no need to stop.

They went in and found a twin-engine turboprop cargo plane that looked like it had been in service since before World War Three. A pair of boots was sticking up out of the right-hand engine's partially open shroud and the faint clicking of a socket wrench emerged from within.

"I take back what I said earlier," Helena said. "The boss has clearly lost her mind."

"It can't be as bad as it looks. Hello!"

There was a muffled clang followed by a string of inventive curses as the mechanic kicked his legs and backed himself out of the engine. A grease-covered bald head emerged last and he turned to peer at them.

Daisuke waved and offered a friendly smile. It would've been more effective coming from Helena, but she appeared too horrified to speak.

At last the mechanic said, "You two the aid workers headed down under?"

They shared a look. Aid workers was a new one, but whatever. The cover story didn't really matter since aid workers were no more welcome in Australia than any other outsider.

"That's right," Daisuke said. "We're in a bit of a rush. Any idea when we can take off?"

"Let me secure this shroud and change out of these greasy coveralls and we'll be good to go. Find yourselves a spot inside to hunker down. Gonna be a long trip."

"How long?" Helena asked.

"Twenty-four hours or so. Gotta stop to refuel and catch some shut-eye in New Delhi."

"Where do you land to refuel for the return trip?" Daisuke asked.

"Tasmania. It's a free trading post. I'll be there for a month. If you two can't magic your way out, come find me." He winked and climbed down a ladder to the hangar floor.

When the mechanic had disappeared into what Daisuke assumed was a bathroom he asked, "How much do you think he knows?"

"Enough to be useful and not a bit more. Good to know we have a backup escape route at least. Come on." Helena led the way up the boarding ramp.

Daisuke gave a little shake of his head and followed. He'd thought jumping out of the plane would be the worst part, but leaving this clunker behind would be a relief.

Despite its unimpressive appearance, the cargo plane, or Puddle Duck, as the mechanic-slash-pilot named it, flew far smoother and quieter than Daisuke had dared hope. The sleeping arrangements in the hold, on the other hand, were every bit as miserable as he feared. They got canvas hammocks that were hung up over cargo crates that had been strapped down tight. The only way Daisuke got to sleep was to use a self-hypnosis spell.

After an eight-hour layover in New Delhi, they were airborne again. That was hours ago and by his estimation they should be getting close to the target location. Helena was busy checking the oxygen cylinders. He knew a spell that would let them breathe despite the thin atmosphere, but the cylinders were a simpler way to go. Outside it was pitch black. Good timing since they'd be that much less apt to be noticed at night.

"Fifteen minutes!" the pilot—the guy never did bother to introduce himself—shouted back from the cockpit.

Helena straightened and handed Daisuke a mask with a tube leading to a valve at the top of a cylinder. "Ready?"

"Yeah, no problem. Just make sure you don't let go of my hand."

"We're about to jump out of a plane without parachutes and you're the only one that knows the flying spell. Nothing's going to get me to let go of your hand." She looked away then back. "You never asked me about my relationship with Carter."

Daisuke cocked his head. "None of my business. Whatever happened between the two of you is between the two of you. Unless there's something you think I need to know, in which case I'm happy to listen."

"I thought you might be jealous."

He almost laughed then caught himself when he realized she was serious. Did she think their relationship was more than friends happy to be alive having sex? If so, that was something they were going to have to discuss at some point.

"This is it!" the pilot shouted. "Opening the hatch."

But not now.

Daisuke strapped the mask over his face and clipped the cylinder to his belt. When he held out his hand, Helena took it, lacing her fingers with his.

A vibration ran through the hull as the loading ramp lowered. The roar of the engines fought with the screaming wind to see which would deafen him first.

He gave a tug on Helena's hand and they ran until the hull vanished under their feet.

Daisuke enjoyed free fall for fifteen seconds, but when Helena's grip got close to breaking his hand, he cast the flying spell.

They didn't actually slow, but he sensed the magic take hold and if he'd wanted to, bringing them to a complete stop would only take a few seconds. However, he wanted to get to the ground with as little effort as possible, which meant free-falling until they were about five hundred yards above the ground.

Helena must have sensed the magic kick in as her bone-crushing grip loosened until it was only uncomfortable.

The screaming wind made conversation impossible. With nothing better to do, Daisuke scanned the ground for the Circle homing spell. It was a spell known only to Circle wizards that created a beacon in the ether that you could only see if you knew the correct revealing spell.

He spotted it at what he guessed was a couple miles to their left. Daisuke nudged Helena who had her eyes squeezed shut. When she opened them, he pointed toward the beacon.

She nodded and he used the flying spell to guide them in the correct direction. They were about a thousand feet in the air and starting to slow when they reached a spot almost directly above the target. The beacon was in the center of a little camp that featured a pair of tents, a few crates stacked up off to one side, and a pair of folding chairs.

Talk about roughing it.

The only light came from a campfire and it didn't reveal much.

There's something moving in the dark. I count ten figures trying to surround the camp and none of them look human.

As a demon, Ruq's night vision was far superior to any human's.

Daisuke slowed them even more, enough that he could speak to Helena without shouting. "Ruq says there's something in the dark and I doubt they're friendly. Are you good to cast a light spell? I'll hover a hundred feet above the camp. We should be able to pick off whatever they are from there."

"I'm ready when you are."

Daisuke frowned as they got closer to the ground. He should be able to sense some corruption by now. Its absence implied whatever they were dealing with, they weren't demons or undead.

"What's the hold-up?" Helena asked.

"Do you sense any corruption?"

"Now that you mention it, I don't."

"I'll handle the light. Binding magic is your specialty. Think you can get them all without killing them?"

"I can try. Depending on how powerful they are, they might resist."

The creatures are only fifteen feet from the tents.

"On three. One, two, three." Daisuke conjured spheres of light and hurled them into the night.

The creatures stood as tall as a man but hunched over. They were covered in long, black hair, their hands ended in rending talons, and their mouths were elongated and filled with fangs. Their eyes glimmered yellow in the dark.

He barely had time to register all that before Helena's magic hit them. Bands of white light formed, binding their arms and legs and sending them crashing to the dirt.

All but one, anyway. That one shattered the bands and turned to run.

Daisuke hit it with a weak burst of black lightning. It crashed to the dirt and didn't rise. That wouldn't have even scratched a thrall, much less a true demon. Whatever they were, they weren't especially strong.

Daisuke came in for a landing just as a slim black woman emerged from one of the tents. He guessed she was around twenty, with a nice figure and wide, scared eyes. She looked from the bound monsters, to Daisuke and Helena, and back again as if not sure what to make of it all.

"Ms. Spencer?" Daisuke asked.

"That's right. How do you know who I am?"

"My name is Daisuke Kugo and the lovely lady beside me is Helena. We're Carter's coworkers. When he missed his last two contact windows, our employer sent us to see what was going on. As for your other evening guests..." Daisuke shrugged. "No idea."

The look of relief that washed over her face might've been comical under different circumstances. "Thank heaven. I've been so worried since Carter didn't come back. He told me to stay here and keep my head down. I've still got plenty of supplies, but five days out here alone is a long time. And you can call me Justine."

"Any thoughts about our hairy friends?" Helena asked. "I can't keep them bound forever."

"Why did you capture them in the first place?" Justine asked. "They're monsters."

"Yes, but they're not corrupt." Daisuke walked over to the nearest creature and crouched beside it. The brute snarled and bared its fangs at him.

He looked closer and found ether running through its body. Looked like a spell of some sort. Certainly nothing he'd seen before. Maybe he could dispel it.

Gathering power of his own, Daisuke passed a hand over the creature. As he did, he pulled the ether running through its body out. It was like the root of an especially long weed, but eventually he got all of it.

When he did, the monster shrank, most of the hair vanishing along with the claws and fangs. What remained was an unconscious, naked black man covered in white markings that meant nothing to Daisuke.

Curious now, Daisuke went from monster to monster, repeating the process until all of them had returned to their human form and he was thoroughly tired. He dragged the one that tried to run back to his fellows and slumped onto one of the supply crates.

"What do you make of them?" Helena asked.

Daisuke shook his head. "No clue. I've never seen a spell like that. My guess is some kind of curse. The way they transformed made me immediately think of a werewolf, but I'm not aware of lycanthropy being a problem in Australia."

"Given how closed off they are, would we even know if it was?" Helena asked.

"Fair point."

"These markings are the same as the ones Carter and I were studying." Justine was kneeling beside one of the unconscious men. "These must be descendants of the tribe that left them."

"Great, what do they mean?" Daisuke asked.

"We never figured that out. Carter was interested in one marking in particular, especially its origin, but I wanted to decipher the entire message. However, it seems like this tribe's symbology is totally different from anything we had in the university library." She looked up, beaming. "Isn't that exciting? If I can decipher it, I'll get my doctorate for sure."

Daisuke didn't especially care about Justine's educational prospects. "Can you show us where you found the markings?"

"Sure, the cave isn't that far. Carter said we should make camp a little ways away just in case anyone was spying on us. I thought it was a silly precaution, but now I'm not so sure. What are we going to do with them?" She nodded toward the still-unconscious men.

"I don't suppose you have enough rope to tie them all up?" Daisuke asked.

Justine shook her head. "Afraid not."

"Guess I could earth bind them," Helena said.

"Perfect, thanks."

Helena pointed then made a fist. The men sank into the ground up to their necks and it hardened into rock. They wouldn't be going anywhere.

"So, what happens now?" Justine asked.

"Between jumping out of a plane and dispelling all those curses or whatever they were," Daisuke said, "I'm about done in. I vote we rest until morning then consider our options."

When Helena didn't object, Justine said, "You two are welcome to share Carter's tent. I don't think I can sleep, so I'm going to check some reference books. Maybe there's mention of these things in the historical record."

Daisuke nodded but wasn't optimistic. He slipped into the second tent and frowned. There was only a single narrow cot. Even snuggled up there was no way the two of them would fit.

"You get the floor," Helena said. "By the way, I really should be in charge of this mission. I've got a year more experience than you."

Daisuke shrugged and dropped to the canvas floor. "If you want to be in charge, it's okay with me. I usually work alone and just did what I do. If I overstep, just tell me."

"It's fine. In fact, the more I think about it, maybe you should take the lead. I'm worried about Carter and that might cloud my judgement."

"You're a professional." Daisuke lay down and put his hands behind his head. "I'm confident you can keep your feelings separate from your job."

"I'm glad *you* are. We were close once, really close. If he's dead..."

"Don't jump to conclusions. We know so little for sure that any guess you might make is apt to be wrong. At first light we'll see what our guests have to say for themselves, then we can decide our next move. Together."

"Thanks, Daisuke." She held out her hand and he gave it a

squeeze. "A lot of guys wouldn't take this situation as well as you are."

The way she said it once again made him think she believed there was more to their relationship than he did. Well, this was hardly the place to discuss it. "Let's get some sleep."

Ruq, make sure nothing sneaks up on us.

Never fear, Master. I'll be on guard.

He closed his eyes and prayed that Helena would forget about the matter by morning.

CHAPTER FOUR

The canvas floor of a tent didn't make for the most comfortable bed, but Daisuke had been so tired he fell asleep almost at once. What woke him was the smell of frying bacon. He sat up and winced at the crick in his neck. A quick burst of light magic took care of that. He glanced at Helena, but she was still sound asleep.

Should he wake her? Maybe not yet.

He pulled his shoes on and stepped out into the bright morning light. Justine was busy cooking bacon in a huge cast iron pan over the coals. An order of pancakes would've been glorious, but he seriously doubted he'd be getting any.

"Morning," he said. "Smells good."

"Thanks. I'm not the greatest cook, but I can manage bacon, eggs, and fried bread." Justine pointed at one of the crates. "There're flasks of water inside. Help yourself. I'm afraid we don't have anything else to drink besides coffee."

"I hate coffee. Don't worry, water's fine." He went over and found a stainless steel half-gallon flask. There were six more inside. He took a swig, swished it around, and swallowed. "Did our guests say anything?"

"I think they're still out."

Daisuke doubted that. And if they weren't awake by now, they might not ever wake up again. He'd worry about that after breakfast. He grabbed a second flask and returned to his tent. A shake of the shoulder roused Helena.

She looked up at him through bleary eyes. "Hi."

"Hi yourself." He handed her the second flask. "Did you sleep at all?"

"Not much. Busy mind. Something smells good."

"It seems Justine is a bit of a cook. Though I've never met Carter, I can confirm that he has excellent taste in women. Shall we eat?"

She rolled out of the cot and stretched, giving him an excellent look at her curves. Even exhausted, rumpled, and unshowered, she was one of the most beautiful women he'd ever seen.

When they went outside, Justine was scooping the eggs out of the bacon grease. Daisuke devoured three along with half a dozen pieces of bacon and four slices of fried bread. He could've eaten all she cooked, but restrained himself.

After they finished, he asked, "How much did Carter tell you about himself and who he worked for?"

"Not a lot. I know he was a wizard and that he was interested in my research. He didn't say anything about his employer beyond the fact that they'd send someone to help if there was trouble. He also didn't tell me why he was so interested in that particular mark. Since magic is involved, I figured I was better off not knowing."

"No doubt about that," Helena said. "Did you find any mention of Aborigine werewolves?"

"I didn't. Not even anything vaguely similar."

"Maybe we should just ask them what's up." Daisuke stood and walked over to the nearest prisoner. "Hey, stop pretending to be unconscious. I've got questions."

The guy ignored him, drawing a frown. "Have it your way."

Daisuke conjured a little spark of lightning from the tip of his finger and tapped the bound man right between the eyes.

He yelped and his eyes popped open.

"Hello, sunshine. Ready to talk now?"

Though clearly awake and aware, the man stared at Daisuke as if not understanding.

"Speak English?"

No reaction save a confused shake of his head.

"Let me try," Justine said. She said something in a strange language and the man nodded and replied the same way.

Daisuke really needed to master a translation spell. Since he already spoke English, German, Japanese, Demonic and Angelic, he'd never bothered to learn it. This was the first time it had caused him an issue.

You could just read his mind, Master.

That's tricky. Too much interpretation involved. I might miss something important.

"He says he's a member of the Bedjiri tribe. The last thing he remembers was something attacking him when he was out hunting."

"What attacked him?" Helena asked.

Justine repeated the question, but the prisoner shook his head and gave a long answer. "He didn't see. Two other members of his tribe had gone missing. The only reason he went out of their village at all was a desperate need for meat."

They questioned the rest of the men and got similar answers from each. Between them they represented four different tribes and none of them saw what grabbed them. Not terribly informative, but at least they seemed calm now.

"Should we let them go?" Helena asked.

"We can't exactly leave them like potted plants. Carter said something about wanting to talk to a local shaman. Was it someone from one of these tribes?"

"I don't know," Justine said. "We'd barely begun discussing it when he went missing. The Bedjiri are the closest, so they're probably the ones we'd end up visiting."

"Since we saved one of their hunters, we should get a friendly welcome anyway." Daisuke turned to Helena. "Unless you have more questions, I think we can let them go."

Helena made a lifting motion with her right hand and the tribesmen slowly rose out of the ground. It looked like they were plants growing in fast-forward. As soon as they were out of the ground, one of them waved and the group jogged off into the wilderness.

"So what now?" Justine asked.

"We need to find Carter," Helena said. "I say we go straight to Milden Station and find out what the hell is going on there."

That sounded reasonable to Daisuke. He turned to Justine. "Do you want to join us or stay here?"

"She should stay," Helena said. "If there's something at the station powerful enough to defeat Carter, we won't be able to protect her and ourselves."

"True, but if more werewolves show up, she'll be in just as much danger here on her own."

"I hate to interrupt," Justine said. "But Carter took our

only dune buggy. How are you planning to reach the station? It's three hours away in the buggy, probably two full days of walking."

Daisuke smiled. "I figured we'd turn invisible and fly. I can have us there in half an hour. Assuming no one stole it, we can drive the dune buggy back when we're finished."

Justine ducked into her tent and came back with a set of keys. "These are the spares. It'll be hard for anyone to argue that you can't take it as long as you have these."

"Thanks." Daisuke pocketed them. "So, are you coming or staying?"

"I'll stay. I'd hate to get in your way if there's trouble."

"Okay. As long as you're hanging back, would you mind doing something for me?"

Justine brightened. "Not at all. What do you need?"

"A map of the area with the locations of the cave where you found the symbols and the four tribes who lost hunters marked on it. I want to see how they relate to each other."

"That's a piece of cake. It'll be ready when you get back."

Daisuke smiled. "Thanks."

He held out his hand and Helena took it. "I'll handle flight if you do invisibility."

"Deal."

At his mental command, the pair lifted off the ground. A faint tingle ran through him as Helena's spell settled over them. A moment later they were zipping across the flats far faster than any dune buggy ever dreamed of going.

Hopefully they'd find Carter alive somewhere at the station.

Who was he kidding? At this point, even finding a body was a dim prospect.

CHAPTER FIVE

Milden Station might well have been the most rundown collection of shacks Daisuke had ever seen. Not that there were that many of them. He counted a dozen during a quick recon flight. A handful of people were moving around, most of them heading toward the largest and sturdiest building, a two-story, tin-covered super shack.

Daisuke landed them a hundred yards outside of town and Helena released her invisibility spell. As they started trudging down the dusty road Helena said, "I didn't have high expectations, but this is ridiculous. Where would you even keep a prisoner? I could kick down most of these shacks, no magic needed."

"Did you spot Carter's dune buggy? I saw no sign of it."

"You think he took off somewhere else and didn't let Justine know?"

"I can't say what he would or wouldn't tell Justine, but there's no way Carter would've missed two contact windows were he able to call. I fear whoever got him, loaded him into the dune buggy and took both of them heaven knows where."

Helena winced. "I hadn't even considered that possibility. I was so sure we'd find him here. Just goes to show you where my brain is."

"I could well be wrong. Some thief might've hotwired the dune buggy and made off with it. Surely someone here knows what happened. Assuming they'll tell us."

Helena clenched her fist. "They'll tell us."

Daisuke grinned. He wasn't used to playing good cop. He shaded his eyes. It had to be eighty already and the sun had only been up for a couple hours. It was going to be miserable today, he just knew it.

They reached the first tin shack, but no one poked their head out as they passed. Daisuke led the way to the biggest building, since it seemed to be some kind of meeting place. Two gray-haired, shirtless fellows were sitting on crates playing checkers. They looked up at Daisuke and stared as if they'd never seen a Japanese man before.

And maybe they hadn't. Given Australia's stance on visitors, Daisuke might be the first to visit since the country sealed its borders. Well, whatever. These two were as good as any to start their investigation.

"Morning, guys," Daisuke said. "We're looking for a friend of ours—white guy, dark hair, a little bit taller than me. He came on a dune buggy a couple days ago. We got worried when he didn't make it back. Have you seen him?"

They both shook their heads, whether to indicate they hadn't seen him or that they didn't understand, Daisuke wasn't certain.

Look at them through the ether, Master. Someone put a spell on them.

Daisuke shifted his vision and sure enough a faint ethereal glow surrounded both their heads. He'd never seen a spell just like it, but guessed it was either mind control or memory modification. He debated dispelling it, but decided against doing so. It would only alert whoever put the spell in place that a wizard had come calling.

Good eye. Thanks for the heads-up.

Helena took a step toward the pair, fist raised.

Daisuke caught her arm and whispered, "They're under a spell."

Her eyes narrowed. "I don't recognize it."

"Me either. Let's go inside and see if anyone else is in any condition to be more cooperative."

"What if they're not?"

"Then we'll have to pick someone and make some modifications. Don't worry, I have no intention of leaving here with nothing."

"Good, because I'm not either."

They left the men outside to their game and pushed through a pair of old-fashioned swinging doors. The inside looked like a combination general store and bar. It kind of reminded Daisuke of the place he'd dropped on Cristo's head back in Japan, though it was in far rougher shape.

Two more black men were playing dominoes at one of the four tables dotting the floor. A single white guy dressed in ragged shorts and a tank top sat at the bar drinking from a dark-brown bottle. There was no bartender to be seen, only a cooler that rattled harder than the Puddle Duck during takeoff. A glance through the ether confirmed that all the men inside were under the effects of the same spell.

Daisuke sat on a stool a couple up from the drinker. "Where can I get one of those?"

"The cooler. It's self-serve. Put three bucks in the box on the side and help yourself."

"Thanks." He glanced at Helena who shook her head.

When he had his drink Daisuke returned to his seat. There was a bottle opener hanging from a nail in a post beside the bar and he used it to pop the lid. A single swallow convinced him that he'd wasted his money. It was the most bitter swill he'd had the misfortune to imbibe.

"Quite a system. Doesn't the owner worry about getting ripped off?"

"Nah. If the beer fund comes in light, I just order that much less next time. Eventually I'll get to the point of ordering enough for myself and the rest of these louts can pound sand. I've told them so enough times that no one tries to gyp me anymore. Zac Kelly." He held out his hand and Daisuke shook it.

"I'm Daisuke. My far-more-attractive companion is Helena. I'm hoping you can help us."

Zac chuckled. "My new friend, if you're in Milden Station, you're definitely in need of help. What can I do?"

Daisuke repeated what he told the men outside. "His partner's getting nervous and she asked us to look into it. We're colleagues of his."

"Sorry, mate, haven't seen anyone meeting that description and the only dune buggies belong to locals. Maybe your friend moved on in the hope of finding a new partner."

"I hate to think Carter would do that, but you might be right. Is there a sheriff or anything hereabouts we might ask? I assume if his body turned up, someone would be notified."

"If a body was found, someone would tell me and I'd call the territorial police. Eventually they'd send someone to take a look. I haven't heard a thing."

"Well, shit. Looks like it's back to square one." Daisuke shook his head and took another sip of the nasty beer. "One last question then I'll get out of your hair. Who cast the spell on you?"

Zac stared just long enough for Daisuke to rip the spell out of his brain. He gave a full-body shudder and tried to fall off his stool.

Daisuke caught him and lowered him gently to the ground.

Master, something's happening.

He looked up from Zac in time to see the two black fellows standing and walking their way. Daisuke hadn't noticed before, but both men were carrying machetes, chipped, rusty ones that would've looked right at home in a horror movie.

The door opened and the two from outside entered. One carried a hatchet and the other a kukri. They moved more like zombies than men and even at full speed, those weapons had no hope of hurting him and Helena.

The spell in their brains had flared brighter, eliminating any confusion about the cause of their current behavior.

Helena made a little circle with her right index finger and white bands of energy appeared, wrapping the would-be killers up and binding them in place.

"Let's dispel the enchantments," Daisuke said. "Maybe when they recover they can tell us something useful. Ruq, head outside and see if we've got more company coming. If the wizard responsible for all this ensorcelled the entire town, we're going to be busy."

Not that busy. I doubt there could be more than twenty humans in the settlement.

"Why would anyone go to so much trouble to control this

miserable little toilet?" Helena asked as she yanked the ether out of a domino player's brain.

Daisuke shrugged. "Beats me. We can add it to the many questions to which we have no answers."

Master, I was wrong. There are twenty-five humans in this town and all of them are headed our way.

"Ruq says the rest of the locals are coming by for a visit."

"We're finished in here, let's go deal with them."

While he appreciated her enthusiasm, dispelling that many enchantments would take a considerable toll. "Use earth bind. I think I finally figured out the point of all this. The wizard wants us to wear ourselves out on his servants so we'll be weak when the counterattack comes."

"Sneaky. Binding that many would do me in. I'm just going to conjure a sinkhole."

He nodded. Daisuke didn't especially care how she did it, as long as the people were secure and unharmed. While he had no problem killing people that deserved it, these folks were victims as much as Carter.

They stepped outside. The crowd, to a person, were filthy and ragged, and armed with hand tools of various sorts. Only twenty yards separated them from the general store and they were closing fast.

Helena raised her hands and ether streamed from her fingertips. The energy outlined a circle that surrounded everyone. The moment it closed, the ground collapsed, sending the townsfolk crashing into a fifteen-foot-deep pit.

Two were close enough to the edge that they didn't fall, but a nudge from an ethereal hand shoved them over, out of sight.

"Problem solved." Daisuke grinned. "Let's get out of the

sun. Hopefully someone will wake up soon and be able to tell us what the hell is going on in this town."

Carter Monk woke up in a deep, dark cavern lit by eerie, floating bugs that glowed greenish yellow. He was lying on the hard stone floor, bound hand and foot by webs made of shadow. Worst of all, try as he might, he couldn't touch the ether. The shadow webs' corruption totally blocked him. They also sapped his strength, leaving him weak.

On the plus side, when the darkness claimed him that night in Milden Station, he hadn't expected to wake up at all. Bad as his situation was, it certainly could've been worse.

The weirdest part was that he felt neither hunger nor thirst and had no need to use the bathroom. He felt certain a few days at least had passed, which made his physical situation all the odder.

Faint clicking drew his attention and he forced himself to roll over. The woman in black was striding right at him. She was dressed exactly as before in the black slit dress that seemed designed to show off her ample curves. Her long dark hair hung loose to the middle of her back and she wore four-inch heels that looked terribly impractical for someone that lived in a cave.

This was the first time he'd seen her since that first night and he wasn't at all certain what to expect.

She stopped a few feet away and stared down at him. "I suppose you're wondering why I didn't kill you."

"That's certainly at the top of my list of questions. Not that I don't appreciate it."

"There are ways to tell when someone has been killed. If whoever sent you to my town found out you were dead, I feared they might not come looking for you. Basically, I kept you alive to act as bait."

"How did that work out for you?"

"Well, someone showed up at Milden Station this morning. They very gently dealt with the humans under my control. They didn't kill a single one. Not exactly the sort of behavior I expected from anyone that might dare challenge me."

"Meaning no disrespect, miss, but I didn't even know you existed until you attacked me. It's equally possible that whoever showed up works for my company and is only interested in finding me rather than fighting you."

Her bloodred lips turned down in a frown. "I hadn't considered that possibility. Keeping you as bait only to catch the wrong fish would be annoying. My initial assumption was that whoever sent you had a deeper plan, but I suppose it's equally possible they used you as a dupe on the off chance you succeeded in killing me."

Carter could practically see the wheels spinning in her mind. He knew far too little about the current situation to make an even remotely educated guess.

"Did you see who arrived?" he asked. "If you describe them, I could probably tell you if they were coworkers of mine."

"Why would you offer to help me?" She sounded suspicious. Not surprising given the current circumstances.

"I think of it less as helping you and more as helping myself. I very much want to get out of this alive. I'm also pretty sure your enemies used me, which makes me sympathetic to your situation. As far as I can tell, there's no actual reason for us to fight."

She made a gesture that encompassed her entire body. "Many humans would fight me simply because of what I am."

Carter tried to shake his head, but lacked the strength to even manage that. "I don't know what you are, but I seldom fight anyone unless they're trying to kill me or set demons loose on the world. What do you say? Can we try working together?"

"Two humans arrived in Milden, a pale, pretty blond woman and a slim man with dark hair and oriental features. They captured most of my servants and dispelled the magic that controls some of the others."

"I recognize both of those people. The woman is likely Helena and the man Daisuke. They both work for the same company I do. I'm sure our boss sent them when I missed my last call-in."

"Are they strong?"

"Helena isn't quite as strong as me. Daisuke... You don't want to fight Daisuke if you can avoid it. He's a nice kid, but there's a cold streak a mile wide in him. If you attack him, he'll kill you and he won't feel bad about it."

"Having seen my shadow magic, you believe this human boy is a match for me?"

"I don't know enough about either of you to say for sure, but I do know that if it came to a fight, I wouldn't last two minutes against Daisuke if he went all out. That said, he is reasonable. If you talk to him and explain the situation, a peaceful solution is possible."

"I'll wait until dark to leave. In the meantime, I will consider your words. It would be unfortunate having to waste more of my time on ignorant dupes." She turned and walked away.

Carter watched her until she disappeared into the darkness. Would she do the smart thing? For his sake and hers, he hoped so.

CHAPTER SIX

Daisuke sipped tepid water from a battered tin cup. Though far from pleasant, it was a vast improvement on the beer. He'd drawn it from the bathroom sink, since it was the only faucet in the place. The store was getting warmer all the time and there was no air-conditioning.

He'd tried to call the boss earlier, but neither his phone or Helena's had a signal. Carter probably had a satellite hookup back at his camp. When the boss mentioned that the Circle had a dedicated satellite, he'd been quite surprised to say the least. No mention was made of how she managed to secure one much less get it into orbit. Assuming, of course, that Crystal hadn't just hacked an existing satellite and stolen it.

In the middle of the store, Helena was busy pacing around the tables. He had seldom seen her this anxious. She must really be worried about Carter.

Zac's groan drew his attention to the store owner. He rolled over and tried to sit up. Bloodshot eyes squinted up at Daisuke, prompting him to wave.

"Bloody hell, mate. My head feels like a grenade went off inside it. How much beer did I drink?"

"I have no idea how many you drank before we arrived, but you only had one that I saw. Your headache is likely the result of me removing the mind control spell someone put on you."

Zac stared at him without comprehension.

"Any of this ring a bell?"

"I remember the beer. No idea about any mind control magic. Other than a couple local shamans, there isn't a wizard this side of Sydney."

Daisuke explained about the station and what they found. "I'm afraid you're mistaken about the lack of wizards. Clearly there's at least one around here somewhere and a strong one at that. We were hoping you could tell us what's going on, now that I've removed the mental magic."

"Wish I could, really. Thing is I don't remember anything strange. If something happened, it would stand out. I mean, nothing ever happens here."

Helena stalked over and he hoped she didn't try and beat some answers out of the poor fellow. It wasn't his fault he had his memories modified.

"Let's come at this from a different direction," she said. "What do the people around here do for a living? Maybe you got into something you shouldn't have."

"I run the store. Most of the others work the opal mines to the north. They get just enough stones to make it worth sticking around. Not that anyone has any better options."

"If they're miners, how come no one is out mining?" Daisuke waved at the still-unconscious men. "These four look able-bodied enough to work. Surely they should be doing something besides playing checkers and dominoes."

Zac's face twisted up. "I can't remember. I know there are mines, but I can't actually remember where they are or the last time anyone went to them. They must have. There's nothing else around here to do for a living. Why can't I remember?"

"The gaps in your memories are certainly from the spell." Daisuke pursed his lips as he thought. "Five will get you ten that someone stumbled onto a wizard's lair during their excavations. Rather than kill the unlucky person and draw more attention, he erased all your memories and placed control spells on you so that you'd attack anyone that caused trouble."

"Then what are we waiting for?" Helena asked. "We need to investigate those mines."

Daisuke shook his head. "Going in blind to an enemy base isn't the best idea. Besides, if I'm right, the wizard will be coming to us soon enough."

"If he's got Carter..."

"If he's got a hostage and we attack, how do you suppose that will go for Carter?"

Helena grit her teeth and growled in the back of her throat. "Badly. I just want to be doing something!"

"I know you do, believe me. The problem is, we're not in a strong position. I don't say this lightly, but the truth is, if Carter's alive, our arrival in town isn't likely to get him killed. On the other hand, if we show up in the wizard's home, that might. I say we give the wizard a day to make his move. If nothing happens, then we search the mines. Sound good?"

"Sounds terrible, but you're probably right."

"I don't know what the hell's going on," Zac said. "But could someone help me up? I need another beer."

Daisuke smiled and pulled the man to his feet. He found he'd taken a shine to the shopkeeper. Hopefully nothing would happen to get him killed.

The sun was starting to set when Daisuke finished picking the magic out of the last townswoman's brain. He'd gotten quite good at it by now and after the first few he found it didn't take that much energy if he finessed it rather than using raw power. He lifted the final victim out of the pit Helena made and two of the locals that had already recovered carried her off, presumably to whichever shack served as her home.

Daisuke was glad to have something to take his mind off the current situation, especially Helena's incessant pacing. He tried to think if there was anyone in his life that he cared about enough to get that upset over them going missing. His mother was the only one that came close and they'd drifted so far apart over the last ten years, he wasn't completely sure even her kidnapping would affect him that badly.

Maybe there was something wrong with him.

Ruq appeared and landed on his knee in rat form. "Would losing me not upset you, Master?"

"It would, but since you're my familiar, I'd know your status at least. I think not knowing if Carter is alive or dead is bothering her more than anything."

With a little rat shrug, Ruq said, "I'll never understand humans. Want to play a game of checkers?"

"Do you even know how to play checkers?"

"Having seen the humans playing it earlier, I'm confident I can pick up the ru—" Ruq cocked his head.

"I feel it too." Something was stirring the ether in a most unpleasant way.

When the sun had fully set, a circle of darkness appeared directly across from the general store and a decidedly feminine shape rose out of it. When the darkness vanished, a stunning woman in a barely there dress stood facing him. She had pale skin, dark hair, bloodred lips, and inhuman curves. It was like someone gave the word "sex" a humanoid shape.

Helena burst out of the store. "What was…"

She trailed off when she saw the new arrival.

"We have company. Since she didn't attack at once, I assume peaceful contact is possible."

"Is that your way of telling me not to blast her immediately?"

"It's my way of asking you not to."

"Fine, I'll stay here. You go talk to her and I'll cover you."

Daisuke plastered on his best smile, not difficult considering how attractive she was, and ambled over with Ruq perched on his shoulder still looking like a rat.

When ten feet separated them, he stopped and said, "Hello. My name is Daisuke Kugo, pleasure to make your acquaintance."

"You may call me Jinx. This town belongs to me and you've ruined years of work."

Her voice was neither warm nor pleasant. Oh well, you couldn't have everything.

"I'm sure the Australian government wouldn't see it that way. Freeing people from mind control is the sort of thing my partner and I do on a semiregular basis. I believe you met another of my coworkers a few days ago."

Her lips curled up in a smile that made Daisuke weak in

the knees. "I did. He assured me that I didn't want to fight you. He seemed sincere, which is why we're talking right now. What is your business in my territory?"

"We wish to ensure our colleague's safety." Out of curiosity more than anything he decided to take a risk. "We're also looking for an artifact, a bronze cylinder about the size of a child's thermos. It would have a small depression in the top with an arcane symbol inside but be otherwise unmarked."

Jinx shook her head. "I've never seen anything like that. What is it?"

"A demon prison. A group of decidedly unpleasant people are looking for it as well. Should we fail to recover and remove the artifact from the area, you can be sure more people will be coming to cause trouble in your territory."

"Should more people come, I will deal with them as I did your associate."

Daisuke grinned. "That would suit me perfectly well. They're no friends of mine. They're also not weak. I fear you might be in danger should it come to a fight."

She barked a laugh. "You expect me to believe you'd care if I came to harm?"

"We are not, as of this moment, enemies. As long as we're not at cross purposes, perhaps we might even be allies. Would you be willing to return Carter and discuss my proposal?"

"I'll hear you out, but not here. My home is in a cavern to the north. Your friend is there as well. Should we come to terms, you can leave together."

Daisuke nodded. "That is acceptable. Excuse me a moment."

He went back to Helena. "I'm going to get Carter. Her lair

is in a cavern to the north, just as we thought. I'll put up an ethereal marker as soon as I arrive."

"Going with her alone is insane," Helena said.

Daisuke shook his head. "If Jinx was really evil, she would've just killed everyone. Instead she ensorcelled them so they'd stay away from her home. Not what I'd call friendly, but better than the alternative. Besides, if I don't play along, there's no guarantee she won't just kill Carter. See if you can convince Zac to loan you a dune buggy. I don't know what kind of shape Carter will be in."

"Fine, I'll be there as soon as I can. But I still don't like it."

"Neither do I, but this would hardly be the first time we've had to do something we didn't like. See you in a bit." Leaving his disgruntled partner behind, Daisuke walked back to Jinx. He added negative energy protection to his defensive spells and strengthened his personal shield. "I assume you'll handle transportation?"

"Since you don't know where we're going, I'd better." Jinx held out her hand and Daisuke took it without hesitation. Her skin was smooth and cool. The texture suggested she wasn't undead at least. "Ready?"

"As I'll ever be."

Darkness swallowed them up.

A moment later a dim light appeared, revealing a huge, domed cavern. A solitary figure lay on the ground wrapped in what looked like black spiderwebs that glowed in Daisuke's ethereal vision. Beneath the webs Carter appeared unharmed.

"You have great courage or feeble brains to come here with me." Jinx released his hand.

Daisuke smiled. "I might not be the world's greatest genius, but I do consider myself a pretty good judge of character. Nothing you've done screams evil and I've had evil screamed at me a few times. Why don't you walk me through the situation and we'll see if we can't come up with an arrangement that works for both of us?"

"You may be the oddest human I've ever met. Follow me. There's no reason for us to stand while we talk."

"I'm going to put up an ethereal beacon so Helena can find me. We'll have plenty of time to talk before she arrives."

Jinx looked back at him and for a moment he feared she might object. "Go ahead. It'll be better than having her wandering around at random up there."

Daisuke lit the ether up outside, directly above his head. Based on the distance the spell needed to travel, he put their depth at about forty yards. Nowhere near as far down as he expected. That done, he followed Jinx to a little sitting area at the edge of the cavern. There was a table and four chairs.

They sat facing each other.

"It's strange, you know," she said. "Though we just met, I feel like you might actually understand me."

"I'll do my best. Please, tell me your story."

"It's a long one, so get comfortable."

CHAPTER SEVEN

"My sisters and I came to this land long ago," Jinx began. "Before your human war that rained fire on the world. That was barely an inconvenience for us, living underground as we do. It might have even been better had you succeeded in wiping yourselves out completely. But you didn't, more's the pity."

"You're clearly not fully human," Daisuke said. "But your appearance suggests at least some human blood. Would you mind telling me what you are?"

"We called ourselves Shadowen. As far as I know, my sisters and I were the only ones of our kind. Our mother was human and our father a risen demon cast out of Astaroth's hell for the crime of not hating life strongly enough. We lived happily for decades, hidden from the world by Father's magic. He was a shadow demon and could manipulate them to create mazes and traps to deceive the unwary. He could also call shadow servants from Astaroth's hell to fight for him."

"I'm surprised the demon lord would allow it if your father had been cast out."

Jinx's lips twisted in a bitter sneer. "Astaroth cares not in the least who summons his lesser servants as long as it's to have them slay mortals. Death and destruction is all that interests the lords of hell."

"I can't fault your analysis. I've yet to meet a demon or demon worshipper that failed to meet your description."

"Hey!" Ruq said.

"Present company excepted of course." Daisuke nodded toward the rat on his shoulder. "This is Ruq, my familiar. Life force interests him much less than sweets. Please continue."

"After four decades, my mother finally died. When she did, Father left. I don't think he could stand looking at us. We probably reminded him too much of Mother. While we had some skill with magic, it was nothing like his. Eventually humans found us and when they did they saw the demon rather than the human and attacked. We defended ourselves but were eventually forced to flee."

"You certainly chose an out-of-the-way place for your new home."

"That was the idea. In the middle of nowhere, underground, no one would ever find us. Our demonic nature meant we needed little food or water to survive, though we did enjoy tea occasionally as a treat. We lived peacefully for decades until someone else found us."

"The opal miners?"

She laughed. "Hardly. Those weaklings were no threat to us. No, the ones that found us were... something else. I still don't know how they sniffed out our magic, but they did. We fought them when they appeared and many of their servants died. My sisters died with them until I was forced to flee. I hid in smaller caverns, always moving, always on alert, like an animal. It was horrible. I spent years like that before I finally got sick of it and returned. I decided if the hunters tried to kill me again, I'd take as many of them with me as I could. But they never came."

"Why?"

Jinx shrugged. "I wish I knew. When it became clear that a confrontation wasn't imminent, I modified the magic I used to keep the miners away from this cavern so that I'd be alerted whenever a stranger arrived at the station. Your friend was the first to do so since I returned. When it turned out he was a wizard, I assumed the worst and struck. After speaking to him and to you, it seems clear to me that I erred."

"Just so I'm clear, whoever attacked you was human, correct? If Carter being a wizard was what made you suspect him, that means that whoever attacked you were also wizards."

"That's right. They summoned monsters, white wolves that resisted our shadow magic. The wizards controlled them somehow." Jinx let out a long sigh. "I know they'll come for me again. There's no way around it. Maybe they'll kill me this time and I can finally join my mother and sisters."

"You don't have to fight them alone. If you wanted to join our team, I, at least, would welcome you."

She stared at Daisuke as if not believing what she heard. "Why?"

"What do you mean, why?" Daisuke grinned. "Every chance you've had to kill, you chose not to. I admit you were a bit reckless attacking Carter, but in the end you didn't do him any permanent damage. You didn't, right?"

Her bitter smile had softened into something genuine

and warm. "No, though he won't be up to anything energetic for a day or two. I've never met a human like you."

"I take that as a compliment. What say we set Carter free and go find Helena? Can you move around during the day?"

"Of course, I'm not a vampire, after all. My magic is stronger at night, but I'm far from helpless during the day."

Daisuke stood and held out his hand. "I'm looking forward to working with you."

Jinx joined him, reached out, paused halfway, then grabbed his hand. "Likewise."

Carter groaned as strength slowly seeped into his limbs. The pins-and-needles feeling reminded him of when the blood returned to a limb after it fell asleep. Far from pleasant, but he should be back to normal when it was over. At least he hoped so.

He rolled over on his back and stared up at a pair of familiar faces. "Been a while, Daisuke."

Daisuke frowned. "Have we actually met face-to-face? The boss told me about you, and Helena expanded on what little I knew, but I don't remember talking to you before."

"I'm not surprised you don't remember. You'd only been with us for six months and we were having a party to celebrate completing a particularly difficult mission. Everyone wasn't there of course, but a dozen members showed up at the store which is a lot for our group. The boss introduced us and pleasantries were exchanged before we went our separate ways. I only remember because you seemed more composed than a young man your age should've been under the circumstances."

"That explains why I don't remember. I'm not much for parties and probably wanted to escape as quickly as possible. Anyway, Carter, let me introduce Jinx. Jinx, this is Carter, my coworker."

The woman, for lack of a better word, offered a little bow. "I apologize for attacking you. Your presence surprised me, but that's really no excuse. I hope you can forgive me."

Carter had been in this game for long enough that little surprised him anymore, but an apology from the shadow magic user that attacked and took him prisoner certainly made the list. The fact that it seemed sincere was the biggest surprise of all.

"Sure, um, apology accepted. I'd really like to get out of this cavern if at all possible."

"That's the plan. Helena should be waiting on the surface." Daisuke offered his hand. "Are you strong enough to stand?"

"One way to find out." Carter grasped the proffered hand and heaved himself up. His knees wobbled and he nearly fell right back on his ass.

"I'm going to call that a no." Daisuke conjured an ethereal disk. "Make yourself comfortable.

Carter gratefully sat. Much as he hated looking weak, trying to force himself to walk would be the height of stupidity. He doubted his magic was up to strengthening him any more than his body was up to running a marathon.

"The enervation spell will wear off in a couple hours," Jinx said. "Unless you have someone skilled at healing, there's really no way to rush the process."

Carter waved a hand. "I'll be fine. Let's just get out of here."

Jinx took the lead, guiding them through a tunnel

whose entrance Carter hadn't even noticed. It curved and twisted before finally emerging onto the alkaline flats. A pair of opal mines, their shafts covered by what could easily be mistaken for well roofs, was visible in the distance.

"What's to keep someone from just wandering down to the cavern through that tunnel?" Daisuke asked.

"The forbiddance spell I placed on it will stop most people and my guardian shadows will deal with anyone else."

"Master, Helena is waiting approximately four hundred yards to our right."

Carter glanced at the talking rat perched on Daisuke's shoulder. He didn't approve of wizards taking demon familiars. It was generally a good way to start down the path of corruption. Not that Daisuke had ever asked his opinion.

The trio set out through the dark under a conjured light. There wasn't much to see beyond gray, dead earth in every direction. It really was a desolate landscape save for the mines.

"How's Justine?" Carter asked.

"She's fine, though worried about you. I've got her working on a project, so hopefully that'll take her mind off of it."

"What sort of project?"

"A map of the local tribes and how they relate to the cave you found." Daisuke explained about the werewolves or whatever they were. "I've never seen magic like what caused their transformation. Are werewolves a problem around here?"

"Not so far as I know," Carter said.

"I've never encountered one in the centuries my sisters and I were here," Jinx added.

"Carter!" Helena's shout ended the conversation and she came running over. "Are you okay?"

Before he had a chance to answer, she was hugging him. As he held her, Carter realized just how much he'd missed Helena.

When they reluctantly separated he said, "I'm fine, just a little weak. Jinx says I'll make a full recovery in a few hours."

Helena turned a hard glare on Jinx. "Why, exactly, is *she* here with you?"

Daisuke gave an abbreviated description of the story Jinx had shared. "Our working theory is that the people that attacked her are the same ones that sent the note to Carter. She's going to team up with us to deal with them. Also, despite our rough introduction, she's a sweetheart. We don't have so many friends around here that we can turn one down."

"Daisuke has been very considerate," Jinx said in a tone so warm and bright that Carter had trouble believing the woman that attacked him had spoken. "And I am sorry about the misunderstanding."

The signs were subtle, a faint crinkling around her eyes and the tightness of her jaw, but Carter knew Helena well enough to recognize the indications of controlled anger. Daisuke, on the other hand, seemed to either not recognize them or not consider them serious.

Helena looked at Carter. "Are you okay with this? You're the one she attacked."

"She apologized and since I suffered little beyond discomfort, I'm content to let the matter go. Given all that we have to deal with, picking an unnecessary fight would be foolish."

"Great," Daisuke said. "Now that we have that sorted out,

let's get back to Justine. I'm sure she's wondering what's happening. We should call the boss at the first opportunity as well."

"I'll take care of it as soon as we get to camp," Carter said.

Helena led them back to where she'd been waiting. Carter's eyes went wide. "My dune buggy! Where did you find it?"

"In a shed behind Zac's store. He said it was an extra and I was welcome to use it. As far as I could tell he had no idea it belonged to you."

"Of course not," Jinx said. "I erased all memories of Carter from the townspeople's minds. It's safer for them not to know if my enemies show up and ask questions."

"Are you seriously going to claim manipulating their memories is a good thing?" Helena demanded.

Daisuke raised his hands before an argument could begin. "Done is done. The question now is, how do we all get back to camp given that it's a two-seat dune buggy?"

"I'll drive Carter and you two can either fly or shadow walk," Helena said.

She held out her arm and Carter eased himself off Daisuke's ethereal disk. His legs were stronger already and he only had to lean on her a little. As soon as Carter was belted in, Helena climbed in the driver's seat and they took off.

After a mile with nothing but the growl of the engine, Carter asked, "Are you okay?"

"Fine."

"Don't give me that. I know you too well. If you're worried about Jinx, I don't think you need to. Her desire to help seems genuine."

"I have no doubt her desire is genuine. Did you see the

way she looked at Daisuke? That little purr in her voice as she spoke to him?"

"I didn't realize you two had that sort of relationship."

She flashed him a look then turned back. "It's complicated."

"Complicated how? Do you love him? Does he love you?"

"I don't know the answer to either of those questions. That's what makes it complicated. And figuring out the answers in the middle of a mission is just asking for trouble we can't have."

"You glaring at Daisuke and Jinx every time they speak to each other isn't going to make the situation any better. Sorting out where you both stand might be the easier option. Not that I'm the best one to be giving relationship advice considering how ours turned out."

"That was my fault. I mistook our work relationship for something deeper than friendship. Maybe I'm making the same mistake with Daisuke."

"Talk to him. We can't plan our next move until I'm recovered and that'll take until morning at least."

She nodded, but Carter had doubts about whether she'd be able to follow through. Despite her professional veneer, Helena was quite emotional. He'd noticed that during her year of training. In retrospect, Carter was honest enough to admit that sleeping with her wasn't the best idea he ever had. At the time, however, it had seemed like exactly the right thing to do.

He swallowed a sigh. Why was life always so complicated?

Daisuke watched the dune buggy shoot away and shook his head. What was Helena's problem anyway? Was she mad that Jinx attacked Carter? While it certainly wasn't the best first impression a person could make, if Carter was willing to let bygones be bygones, it certainly seemed Helena could.

"She doesn't like me," Jinx said. "Not that I blame her after my earlier behavior. Most humans don't like me as a matter of course. I think it's something to do with my demon blood."

"Nah, once Helena gets to know you, she'll come around."

"I'm less certain, Master. Despite my charming personality, I still don't think she likes me. Perhaps she's prejudiced against demons."

"You're a giant talking rat who regularly covers yourself in ice cream just so you can lick it off. Helena nearly threw up the first time she saw you do that. She dislikes you because you're disgusting, not because you're a demon."

"That doesn't make me feel better."

Jinx giggled and quickly slapped a hand over her mouth. "Sorry. I didn't mean to laugh at you. It's been so long since anything made me smile, much less laugh."

"I laugh at Ruq all the time, so feel free to join in. Now, do you want to fly or shadow walk?"

"Father could fly, but I never managed the spell."

"Would you like to?" Daisuke held out his hand.

She looked at his hand for a moment before taking it. "I would."

Daisuke grinned and shaped the ether. The next thing he knew they were airborne.

Jinx let out a whoop and smiled at him, her eyes glowing slightly red. She seemed like a normal woman just then. And really, when you got right down to it, that's what she was. Only a coincidence of birth made her a half demon. And her father had been a risen demon, so not even really evil.

"This is wonderful!" With her hair streaming behind her, Jinx looked more like an angel than a demon.

They flew along right above the dune buggy. After a few minutes Daisuke noticed it was taking less effort to extend his spell to Jinx than it had to Helena. The ether flowed between them much more easily.

It's because she's an inherently magical being. Demons, angels, and spirits are all natural conduits for the ether.

That was surprisingly informative for Ruq.

I'll have you know that just because I'm a glutton, it doesn't mean I'm an ignorant one.

The thought never crossed my mind.

It took a couple hours to return to camp at the dune buggy's pace. Not that Daisuke minded. Jinx's joy at flying was infectious and he found himself grinning the whole way back. When they landed beside the dune buggy, she leapt into his arms and hugged him.

"That was glorious, thank you."

He hugged her back. "I'm glad you enjoyed it."

"Are you two having fun?" Helena asked.

Jinx let go and turned to face her. "I was."

Helena's right hand balled into a fist, but she relaxed it at once. "I'm so happy for you."

"Thank you." Jinx smiled, drawing a growl from Helena.

"Welcome back, Carter." Justine had emerged from her tent and hurried over. "Are you okay?"

"I'm much better than I was." Carter got out of the dune buggy without any help and walked around to hug Justine. "Good job holding down the fort."

The hug was completely chaste and Daisuke revised his theory about the pair's relationship. It looked more like friends or maybe mentor and mentee.

Daisuke introduced Jinx to Justine. After another apology the two women shook hands. Justine, at least, seemed like she was going to be reasonable.

"Not to be rude," Carter said. "But I'm all in. See you in the morning."

He ducked into his tent and a moment later the cot creaked.

"That's one tent down," Daisuke said. "How do we want to handle the sleeping arrangements?"

"I only need eight hours of sleep a week," Jinx said. "So I'm good out here."

"I've slept on the ground plenty of times," Daisuke said. "If you've got a spare blanket I can spread on the ground, I'll be fine out here as well. But first I need to eat."

"I don't mind sharing my tent," Justine said.

Helena looked from Daisuke to Jinx then back. What, exactly, she thought was going to happen if she went into the tent, he could easily imagine. What was actually going to happen, on the other hand, was him eating whatever he could find in the larder and going to sleep.

"Want something to eat?" Daisuke asked.

Helena shook her head. "I had a snack at Zac's store before I left to pick you guys up. Guess I'll sleep in Justine's tent. See you in the morning."

The two women ducked into the tent. Daisuke popped open a large, air-tight container and studied his options. Everything was remarkably healthy and sugar free. He settled on ham, bread, and a couple apples. There was also a kettle which he filled from one of the water flasks and set over a conjured fire. Next he grabbed a pair of tin mugs and two tea bags.

"There isn't a single cookie," Ruq said. "How will I survive?"

"I'm confident you can gut it out. It's not like you actually need to eat. Unlike me."

Daisuke used a knife he found to slice up the apple and combine it with the bread and ham to make a reasonably tasty sandwich. He glanced over his shoulder at Jinx. "Sure you don't want anything?"

"I require almost as little food as I do sleep." She held up a tan blanket. "Justine tossed this out for you."

"Great." Daisuke carried his sandwich over and sat on the blanket. The tea kettle whistled, prompting him to end the fire spell and pour two cups. He handed one to Jinx. "Not sure if it's your flavor, but I remember you said you liked tea."

Jinx accepted the cup and moisture glinted in her eyes. Daisuke took a bite of his sandwich and said a silent prayer that she didn't start crying. There were few things he liked dealing with less than crying women.

She took a sip and smiled. "It's very good, thank you. Seems like a lifetime since I felt safe enough to enjoy a cup of tea and had someone to enjoy it with."

"I say take your pleasure where you can. In this line of work, you never know which day might be your last." He took a sip of his own tea and grimaced.

"Do you not like it?" she asked.

He chuckled and focused on the sandwich. "As far as I'm concerned, tea is just a vehicle for cream and sugar, neither of which are present in the larder. On its own it reminds me of hot, dirty dishwater."

"Then why did you make it?" Her eyes widened. "Just for me?"

"It's a small enough thing to do. Considering all you've been through, I figured you deserved something nice." Daisuke finished his dinner, took a moment to lay an invisible ward that would keep any of the nasty local wildlife out of the campsite, and lay back on the blanket. "That hit the spot. See you in the morning."

Jinx nodded but couldn't stop staring at the cup of tea in her hands. Daisuke closed his eyes. If she enjoyed the nasty stuff more power to her. For his part, he'd have killed for a hot fudge sundae.

CHAPTER EIGHT

The sound of Helena's and Jinx's voices woke Daisuke from his fitful sleep. Though he'd slept on the ground plenty of times on missions, that didn't mean he enjoyed it or found it pleasant. Rather than open his eyes, he lay quietly and listened.

"Why do you wear such a skimpy dress?" Helena asked.

"This is shadow silk, very difficult to make. My sisters and I worked together to make enough so we could each have a dress. This is the design I came up with for my share of the bolt. Shadow silk's magic lets it transform into shadow when I do. That way I don't solidify naked. That happened a couple of times, but luckily I made it home before turning human again."

"I've never heard of shadow silk."

"As I said, it's very rare. It's literally made of spun shadow. Only shadowmancers can weave it."

"Do you have any plans for after the mission?" Helena asked.

"Not yet. I'm alone in the world. I'm sure something will come up."

Daisuke chose that moment to open his eyes. "Morning. Talk about a nice sight to wake up to. You're both looking lovely."

Jinx's bone-white skin flushed a little at the compliment. Helena just glared at him. Why, exactly, he wasn't certain. In his experience, the women in his life seldom needed a reason to get mad at him. They seemed to do so as a matter of course.

"Who's on breakfast detail?" Daisuke asked. "I'm starving. Oh yeah, did Justine show you the map I asked her to make?"

"I glanced at it, but I'm not sure what you were hoping to figure out." Jinx said.

"I was trying to figure out which tribe controlled the cave where the demon symbol was found. If they drew it, then they must've seen either the prison or the seal. Maybe we'll get lucky and it'll turn out to be the tribe's sacred relic or something."

"If it's a sacred relic, how will we convince them to give it to us?" Helena asked.

"I figured I'd send Ruq in one night to steal it. Then it's a quick shadow walk home and the boss can lock it up in the vault. If she wants, we then keep looking for... What was her friend's name again?"

"Xerxes."

"Right, Xerxes."

Jinx cocked her head. "You'd have no qualms about stealing the tribe's idol?"

"No," Daisuke said. "Better for the tribe, not to mention the world, if we steal it than the others looking for the artifact slaughter them all and take it. And I promise you the

Blood of Solomon would have no compunction about doing so."

"The Blood of Solomon are your enemies?" Jinx asked.

"They're the enemies of all right-thinking people." Carter was standing outside his tent, all signs of the previous day's weakness gone. He'd changed into a fresh pair of khaki shorts and a gray t-shirt. "I'll start breakfast."

"Maybe you'd better let me do it," Helena said. "Unless your cooking has improved in the last three years."

"Has yours?" Carter countered.

This time Carter was on the receiving end of Helena's glare. Daisuke grinned, sat up, and shifted to join Jinx. "Like an old married couple, aren't they?"

"I've never known an old married couple, so I'll have to take your word for it."

"What about your parents?"

"Our family was… unique. Mom was the only one that needed to eat on a regular basis. Dad didn't eat at all and my sisters and I only once a week. Mom just fixed what she wanted and if I or the other girls were hungry, we had some."

"They must have argued." Daisuke thought back on some of Mom and Yoshikazu's arguments. They were weird in that no one ever yelled. They consisted mostly of cold silences.

"Dad never got angry. I think he was afraid if he lost control for even a moment his demonic nature would take over and he might hurt Mom or us."

"He must have loved you all very much to keep such tight control over himself. I would've liked to meet him and your mother." He glanced at Jinx and found her crying again. Daisuke gave her hand a squeeze. "Sorry. I didn't mean to upset you."

"You didn't, not really. I haven't thought about either of

them in a long time. The memories just sort of hit me. Anyway, Dad wouldn't have liked you. He had issues with human wizards."

"What kind of issues?"

"He killed them whenever he met one. I think he had some bad experiences when he was still a true demon."

"If he killed me, it would certainly make it hard for us to talk."

Jinx laughed and wiped her eyes. "It certainly would've. Still, I'd like to imagine that Dad would've made an exception for you."

While Daisuke and Jinx were talking, Justine had emerged from her tent and taken over the cooking duties. The smell of frying bacon filled the campsite as she worked over a magical flame Carter conjured. Daisuke's mouth watered. He hadn't been eating nearly enough. If he wanted to be at his best, that would need to change.

He gave Jinx's hand a final squeeze and hopped to his feet. Carter glanced his way as he approached. "Is Helena really that bad of a cook?" Daisuke asked.

Carter smiled and shifted his gaze to Helena, who was watching Justine get another pan ready for the eggs. "She was three years ago. I assumed you'd know more about it now than I do."

"Why? We don't live together. When we eat together, it's always takeout."

"I assumed you two were a couple. At least judging by her reaction to the attention you've been giving the charming half demon."

"Is that why she's so bent out of shape? I never took her for the jealous type. I guess the boss knows more about her than I do. Speaking of which, did you call her?"

"Yes, before I came out. The demon prison is our priority, but she's still really worried about her friend."

"What about Jinx?"

"She said she trusted your judgement."

Daisuke nodded. He appreciated that he'd earned the boss's trust. Not that there was much she could do halfway around the world if she disapproved.

"Food's ready." Justine passed out bacon-and-egg sandwiches.

Daisuke devoured two in short order and would've happily eaten a third had there been one for the eating. No conversation was had while they ate and as soon as they were done, Carter unfolded a plastic table upon which he spread the map Justine had made.

"Okay, the cave is here." Carter stabbed a spot on the map with his finger. "It's about ten miles north of camp."

Daisuke looked north and frowned. "There are no hills that way."

"No, but there is a valley. The cave is dug into the side of it." Carter tapped the nearest circle. "This represents the Bedjiri tribe. They're the closest and the ones I planned to approach first. I don't even know the names of the other two tribes."

"So what's the plan?" Daisuke asked.

Justine hesitantly raised her hand. "There's another problem. At the rate we're going through food, we'll run out in a couple days."

"Right," Carter said. "I only planned for two of us. I'll contact my brother and tell him we need more supplies. I wanted to talk to him about whoever gave him that note for me anyway."

"Try to get more calorie-dense food," Daisuke said. "I'm

barely maintaining my energy as it is. If we get into a serious fight I'll be in trouble."

"And be sure to get something sweet," Ruq added.

He shot Ruq a look but didn't chastise him. Something sweet would be most welcome.

Carter shifted his gaze to Helena and Justine. "Any other requests?"

They both shook their heads.

"Okay. After I call my brother, I say we head to the cave for a look around then continue on to talk with the Bedjiri shaman. Hopefully he can give us the information we need. If not, we can move on to the next tribe. Justine, you'll have to come with us to act as interpreter. I can use translation magic, but I don't want to risk any misunderstandings by casting a spell without permission."

Carter headed for his tent to use the satellite phone leaving Daisuke alone with the ladies. "So how are we going to handle transportation? I assume Justine will ride with someone in the dune buggy, which means three of us will have to fly."

"Carter knows a version of the flying spell," Helena said. "I'll go with Justine and Jinx can fly with you."

Daisuke frowned. While he enjoyed flying with Jinx, it was still taxing and he preferred to save his strength for the fight he knew had to be coming.

"Don't worry," Jinx said. "I can change into my shadow form and ride in your shadow. I'll be weightless and invisible, so it will add nothing to your burden."

Helena growled a little. "If you can do that, why didn't you do it last night?"

"I wanted to feel the wind in my hair and enjoy the night

sky." Jinx's smile would've curled any man's toes. "It was an amazing experience. I hope to do it again someday."

"Once the mission's complete and I don't have to worry about conserving energy, I'd be happy to take you flying again."

That earned Daisuke another glare from Helena and he remembered, too late, what Carter had said about thinking the two of them were in a relationship. He and Helena needed to talk and no mistake.

Carter emerged from his tent. "He'll be here with supplies in two days. I told him to include plenty of honey as it's the only sweet thing I could think of that would keep."

"That's perfect, thank you," Daisuke said. "Shall we depart?"

Carter conjured what looked like a snowboard made of pure light and stepped on it. The construct rose a foot off the ground. Jinx vanished and he felt a slight chill run down his spine. He assumed that meant she'd merged with his shadow.

"Ruq, stay with Helena so we can communicate."

The imp flew over and landed on the dune buggy's seat directly between Helena and Justine.

Preparations complete, Daisuke cast his own flying spell and they were off.

Daisuke flew a little ways ahead of the dune buggy as they approached the cave. He wanted to get a look at what they were dealing with before Helena and Justine drove up to it. Carter was hanging back and keeping a watchful eye on the ladies. Not that Daisuke thought Helena needed looking after, but if she was attacked and had to protect Justine as well, things might be tricky for her.

Soon enough he spotted the entrance to the valley. It was actually more like a canyon, with high walls and a narrow bottom. A stream ran along the center of it. When the rainy season came, he'd want to be far away from the narrow canyon. Anything in there would get washed away in a hurry.

It didn't take long to spot the cave. Unfortunately, the cave wasn't all he spotted. Six more werewolves like the ones that attacked the camp were milling around outside the dark entrance. Aside from a few drawings, the cave was supposed to be empty, so why would anyone bother to put guards in front of it?

Whatever the reason, he couldn't let the others just drive up on them.

Tell Helena to stop. There are werewolves guarding the cave.

Message sent, Daisuke flew back to join the others. The dune buggy was parked half a mile into the canyon and Carter had already landed. Daisuke joined them and as soon as his feet touched the ground, Jinx emerged from his shadow.

"Are you sure they were werewolves?" Carter asked.

"I'm sure they were the same as the creatures that showed up around your camp the night before last. Whether they're actually werewolves or some other sort of monsters, I can't say with absolute certainty. I am confident that they're liable to object to us entering the cave."

"Then we need to get them out of the way." Carter turned to Helena. "Want to take a run at them? It'll be just like the old days."

"That'll probably be best. If they're like the others, then

removing the curse will restore them to normal. We'll signal when it's safe to approach."

Daisuke nodded. "Good luck."

Carter smiled. "We'll be staying well above the range of tooth or claw."

He conjured the energy board again and Helena climbed on in front of him. Carter put his arms around her and took off.

Daisuke plopped into the dune buggy's driver seat beside Justine. Ruq in rat form promptly crawled up in his lap. "They shouldn't be long."

Jinx moved up to stand beside him. "Does it not bother you to see them fly off like that?"

He looked up at her. "Of course not. Helena told me herself that they used to be close. I pretty much expected the old romance to rekindle."

"Helena probably won't like that either," Justine said.

Daisuke shifted to look at the younger woman. "What won't she like?"

"That you're not upset. A man is expected to at least get annoyed when his girlfriend flies off with another man."

"She's not my girlfriend. More like friends with benefits."

"You should definitely tell her that," Justine said. "Because you two are clearly not on the same page relationshipwise."

"Yeah, I think I'll hold off on that until we're not hunting a demon artifact in the middle of one of the most desolate landscapes I've ever visited."

"The signal, Master."

Daisuke looked up in time to watch a golden flare slowly fading away. Excellent, this conversation was not one he was eager to continue.

Jinx vanished into his shadow and he fired up the dune

buggy. Five minutes later they reached the cave and found six werewolves buried up to their necks in the ground. The monsters snapped and snarled, but otherwise couldn't move.

He parked well away from them and got out. Carter and Helena were standing beside the cave entrance. They looked his way as the group approached and he asked, "No issues?"

Helena shook her head. "I wouldn't want to fight them hand to hand, but they don't seem to have any magic resistance. Whoever made them clearly wasn't worried about wizards."

"Given how few of us there are, most people don't worry about wizards," Carter said. "Let's go inside."

"I hope those things didn't damage any of the pictographs," Justine said as she hurried to join Carter, who had conjured a globe of light.

Helena fell in beside Daisuke while Jinx brought up the rear.

"Sorry to ditch you like that," Helena said. "I know you hate to miss a fight."

Daisuke shook his head. "No worries, as the locals say. I had no doubt you and Carter could handle six werewolves, as long as they were the same as the first batch we dealt with. And I'm happy to save my strength for now."

Carter and Justine had stopped and were staring at a collection of stick figures and squiggles. One of the squiggles was the demon mark. Daisuke shifted his vision to the ether but saw neither magic nor corruption around the sigil. He still wasn't totally sure it was an actual demon symbol and not just a coincidence.

Justine blew out a sigh of relief. "Everything looks okay."

"Have any changes been made?" Daisuke asked.

She shook her head. "Not that I can see. Carter?"

"It looks exactly the same to me as well. I think it's time to head on to the village."

"What about the prisoners?" Helena asked.

"Let's dispel their curses and let them go." Carter led the way back out of the cave.

Aside from dealing with the werewolves, the stop had been a complete bust.

Daisuke went to the nearest one and looked closely at the threads of ether running through its body. He frowned at the dark flecks tainting the spell. This was different. Someone had added corruption to the magic.

He felt the ether shift and looked up in time to see Carter getting to work on a werewolf.

"Stop!"

The warning came too late. The monster roared and howled, thrashing in its prison before going totally still. Daisuke hardly had to look to see it was dead. Over the course of half a minute the werewolf turned back into a shirtless, black-skinned man marked with white symbols.

"What happened?" Helena asked.

"The curse has been altered," Daisuke said. "Whoever cast it added corruption to make removing it lethal."

"What are we going to do about them?" Helena nodded toward the remaining werewolves. "If we just leave them, eventually they'll thrash themselves free."

Daisuke hesitated. Carter was technically in charge of the mission and the most experienced of them by years. Just taking over wouldn't be well received.

"I believe I can help." Jinx wove her hands in circles and darkness gathered around them. A fine black web fell over the werewolf Daisuke had been examining. As soon as it touched the monster it went still. "The webs drain their strength so they won't be able to get free."

Daisuke grinned. "That's perfect, thanks."

"Indeed." Unlike Daisuke, Carter wore a deep frown. "I should've examined him more closely before I began. I killed that man for nothing."

"It was an accident," Daisuke said. "Blame the asshole that cursed him instead."

Carter clapped him on the shoulder. "Thanks. When Jinx finishes, we'd best head on to the village. We have way too many questions and not nearly enough answers."

CHAPTER NINE

B
edjiri Village was in flames when Daisuke spotted it. He and Carter hung in midair watching the smoke swirl in the wind. Helena had stopped the dune buggy as soon as Ruq relayed the request. Now they needed to decide what to do. There were no sounds of gunshots, so whoever had attacked the village was probably using magic.

They were too far away to make out any details and flying in when unknown magic was being flung around was far too dangerous. If it was someone that meant them ill, that would be like waving a giant sign that said "kill me now."

"I'll land a little closer then sneak in for a better look," Daisuke said.

"Dangerous to go alone." Carter shook his head. "I'll come too."

"I've got Jinx with me and we're better at sneaking than you with your flashy light magic. I can relay what's happening through Ruq."

"Fine, just be careful. I don't know what's going on, but

things suddenly seem a lot sketchier than they did when I arrived and I don't like."

Daisuke grinned. "As long as Haakon doesn't show up this will still be less dangerous than my last mission. We'll be back."

He flew onward while Carter descended to join Helena and Justine. While he liked and respected Carter, Daisuke hated having to run his every decision through a superior. That was the main reason he preferred working alone.

A mile further on he landed and Jinx emerged from his shadow. Ahead of them, the dark forms of werewolves could be seen battling some sort of white-furred dogs that glowed with divine energy.

Jinx stiffened beside him. "Those beasts are the same ones that attacked my sisters and me."

"What are they?"

"I have no idea, but they're highly resistant to shadow magic. If it comes to a fight, my powers will be of little help."

"As long as they're fighting werewolves, I'm content to let the beasts have their way. Having seen the evolved curse, I'm not certain that saving these poor people is even possible."

Daisuke passed a description of what was happening back to Ruq. Part of him wanted to get a closer look and another part argued that was a stupid thing to do. Once the fighting was finished, they could see what was what.

There was a stone pillar jutting out of the ground about a hundred yards away. Daisuke ran over to it and lay down on the shadow to keep watch with Jinx beside him.

"I was afraid you might do something rash when you said those were the things that killed your sisters."

"I would very much like to do something rash, but I also understand that I have no hope of winning against them.

Yesterday I wouldn't have cared if they killed me as long I sent them to hell first. Now I find I wish to live."

"Glad to hear it. I wish I had some binoculars. I'd prefer to avoid using magic lest we attract unwelcome attention."

The battle continued for about fifteen minutes before the white dogs finished off the last of the werewolves. Whatever those things were, they had to be strong to kill so many enemies twice their size. Carter was a light magic specialist. Hopefully he'd heard of them. Unknown enemies were always the hardest to deal with.

"To the left, about a third of the way into the village," Jinx said. "Do you see him?"

A figure in a white robe trimmed in silver strode through the still-burning village. The white dogs, once so ferocious, ran over to him—at least Daisuke assumed it was a him—bounding like puppies. White Robe gave them each a pat on the head before continuing his walk through the ruins. He looked left and right, clearly searching for something and just as clearly not finding it.

When he reached the far end of the village, he raised a hand and a white disk appeared. The dogs went through first then the man. Daisuke waited a minute then told Ruq the others could advance.

"Who was he?"

"One of the people that led the attack against us. There are three of them that I saw. Whether there are others that didn't join the fight I can't say. He wielded powerful divine magic."

"Yeah, his Heaven portal made that clear. I guess it makes sense that someone serving the archangels would attack werewolves. Killing half demons that weren't bothering anyone, on the other hand, seems a bit excessive."

When the rumble of the dune buggy's engine reached him, Daisuke stood and waved Helena over. As soon as they stopped and Carter descended to join them, Daisuke made his report. "Any of this ring a bell?"

He directed the question to Carter, but answers from anyone would've been welcome.

"The white-robed wizard isn't familiar to me," Carter said. "But the dogs sound like white wolves, a hunting beast that can be summoned by powerful servants of the archangels. How many did you say there were?"

"I counted four." Daisuke looked at Jinx who nodded her agreement.

"Wow. One wizard summoning and controlling four white wolves is… impressive."

"Could someone summon a white wolf and transfer control to another wizard?" Jinx asked.

"I'm sure they could, why?"

"The person in the white robe and two of his buddies are the ones that attacked Jinx and her sisters," Daisuke said.

"And now they're killing werewolves?" Carter shook his head. "Sounds like whoever they are they're on an extermination mission."

"I've never heard of such a thing," Helena said.

"You have if you studied history, though it's usually one group of humans doing it to a different group." Daisuke scratched his chin. He was going to need to shave soon. "My question is, why here and why now? And most importantly, does it have anything to do with the demon prison?"

"I can't believe any of this is unrelated to the prison." Carter turned toward the still-smoking village. "Let's take a closer look. Maybe some clue was left behind."

No one greeted the suggestion with great enthusiasm, but

they all fell in behind Carter just the same. They reached the first corpse, a naked Aborigine that had his throat torn out. Bite wounds marred both arms and a deep burn covered the left side of his abdomen. A few tribal markings had survived whatever burned him.

Not a pretty way to die.

"This is wrong." Justine knelt beside the body.

"I know what you mean," Helena said. "Even cursed men don't deserve to die like this."

"What?" Justine looked up at her. "No, I mean the markings on his body. They're not Bedjiri. Too many of them have been destroyed for me to say for sure which tribe he came from, but it definitely wasn't this one."

The group entered the village proper. Daisuke wasn't sure what the huts were made from, but it looked like rock. Dried mud, maybe? Maybe they built them at the end of the rainy season. He had no idea about the habits of the local tribes. Nor was he interested beyond finding the demon prison.

Justine went from body to body, checking the markings that survived the mauling they'd taken. The first one was the most intact and a few had been ripped completely to pieces. And it wasn't just men. At least a couple women were among the dead. Justine's lack of squeamishness impressed Daisuke. He knew plenty of people that would've been tossing their guts up at the sight of this mess. And the less said about the smell, the better.

Daisuke checked everything with his magical vision and aside from a few lingering wisps of divine magic, there was nothing. If the prison had ever been here, it wasn't here now. And it hadn't looked like the guy in white took anything with him.

At the far end of the village Justine said, "I found three dead Bedjiri along with corpses from two other tribes. Exactly which ones I can't say. The bodies were too badly damaged. The next nearest ones seem like a safe bet, but that's just a guess on my part."

"I saw nothing magical," Daisuke said. "Did anyone else?"

The other wizards all shook their heads.

"Let's try the next tribe west of here," Carter said. "We should have time to reach them and still make it back to camp before dark."

"When did you say the supplies were supposed to arrive?" Daisuke asked.

"Early the day after tomorrow. Why?"

"I wonder if whoever gave your brother that note is friends with anyone that wears a white robe?" If the white-robe guy and his friends attacked Jinx and she was right about the note being a trick to get her to expose herself, then they had to figure out if Carter's brother was a willing tool or a dupe.

Hopefully it was the latter. Getting set up by your own brother wasn't a nice idea.

CHAPTER TEN

They reached the second village in the early afternoon. It was in just as bad a shape as the last one, maybe worse. The mud huts had been completely leveled and several dozen bodies lay torn and broken on the ground. A few flames still sputtered, but most were down to coals. The man in white must've hit this place before the Bedjiri.

Daisuke shook his head as he slowly landed in a clear space near the middle of the village. He'd seen some awful things over the years, but the slaughter in these villages ranked right up there with the worst. A simple wind spell kept the stink and smoke away and he welcomed the relief.

Jinx appeared beside him. "This is…"

"Yes, it is. Are you okay?"

"That might be an exaggeration, but I'm not about to faint or anything. You know, despite being a half demon, before my sisters and I were attacked I actually lived a fairly sheltered life. I'd never even seen a dead body, other than Mom's. The last few months have been a bit overwhelming."

"I'll bet. You don't need to hang around for this." He sensed Carter getting closer and the roar of the dune buggy grew louder by the moment. "You can stay in my shadow until it's over."

"I appreciate your consideration, but I mean to see this through. If I'm going to avenge my family, something like this can't get the better of me."

Daisuke respected her grit and so said nothing more on the subject. Carter landed a few feet away and the light board he'd been riding vanished.

"It just gets worse," he said. "No survivors?"

"Not that I found. I can't see any lingering enchantments from the werewolf curse." Daisuke knelt beside a severed head for a closer look. "Whether that means they weren't cursed or that the magic doesn't linger after death, I can't tell."

"If the man in white killed normal people," Carter said, "it certainly raises him a notch in the scumbag department. What do you want to bet there's at least one more village just like this?"

"No bet." Daisuke straightened and offered a silent prayer for the dead. "Right now all I want is to find the prison and secure it before these lunatics beat us to it. I thought the Blood of Solomon were bad, but I've never heard of them doing something like this."

Carter grimaced. "I'm sure none of those fanatics would hesitate to commit an atrocity like this should it be necessary, but you're right, I haven't heard of anything just like this before."

Helena and Justine arrived and the latter got to work studying the bodies. Daisuke couldn't help being impressed with her mental fortitude. There weren't many nineteen-year-old college students that could deal with a mess like this as calmly as she did.

Master, there are tracks leading away from the village.

"Ruq found signs that someone escaped. I'm going to take a look."

"I'll come too," Jinx said. He suspected she was more eager to get away from the carnage than anything.

He let Ruq's psychic presence guide him to the south-eastern side of the village. Sure enough a line of scuff marks led out into the wastes. It was impossible, at least for him, to tell exactly what had made the marks, but his guess was werewolves.

See how far they go, but don't do anything foolish.

Rest assured, Master, that I will make my own safety the highest priority.

He fully deserved Ruq's sarcasm. Daisuke knew better than anyone that his familiar wasn't one to take unnecessary chances. But he still felt the need to offer the warning. It was like a father putting his arm in front of his kid in a car despite knowing that it would make no difference in a crash.

Jinx stared out over the dead flats, an introspective look on her face.

"Penny for your thoughts."

"Just wondering what my life will be like when this is over, assuming I live through it of course. It's entirely possible that I'm the only one of my kind in the world."

"You could easily pass for a normal human woman. The only time your demonic nature appears is when you lose your temper or get excited. When that happens, your eyes glow a little red. A pair of magical contact lenses would sort that out. Zurich's a nice city. I'd be glad to help you get settled should you wish it. With your looks, finding work wouldn't be a problem. You could probably be a model."

She looked away and asked, "Why are you being so nice to me?"

"That's a weird question. Why wouldn't I be nice to you? You explained the thing with Carter and under the circumstances I can understand why you were aggressive. Other than that, you've been a helpful, charming companion. I find I enjoy your company a great deal."

"I like you too." She cleared her throat. "I mean I enjoy your company too."

He grinned. A bashful half demon, who'd have thought?

The tracks end half a mile from the village. They just vanish as if they never were.

That's okay. Come on back.

"Find anything?" Carter asked from behind him.

"The tracks just vanish half a mile from here. Any idea what's out there?"

"No clue. The local tribes and that cave were all that interested me around here. It seems that will have to change. Justine found members of three tribes among the dead. The fourth tribe marked on our map doesn't seem to be involved. At least not yet. She didn't really understand why they'd be mingled like this. Seems the tribes seldom gather save for marriages."

"So what's the plan?"

"I thought we'd make a big loop and swing by the third tribe on our way back to camp."

"If you guys can manage without me, I think I'd like to make a scouting trip along the escapees' tracks."

"Good idea. If there's trouble, prioritize withdrawal."

"I will. Oh, be sure to check the gas tank. I don't know

how much one of those things holds, but we've done quite a bit of running around so it must be getting low."

"Shit! I didn't even think about that. Getting stranded out here would not be ideal. Maybe we'll be heading right back to camp after all."

Daisuke nodded. "Either way I still want to take a look around. See you tonight. Are you coming with me, Jinx?"

"Yes," she said at once.

Both the answer and the enthusiasm with which she gave it pleased him. "Then let's go."

"It's a wonder anyone can live out here," Daisuke said as he flew over the vast emptiness.

"You humans are remarkably adaptable." Ruq flew beside him, still invisible but close enough that they could talk aloud. "These tribes have been living out here for how long?"

"Thousands of years, I guess. I wonder if they're even aware that World War Three happened."

"Not if they're lucky. How far are we going? We haven't seen anything for miles."

Daisuke slowed then hovered. They'd left the tracks behind miles ago and there was no sign of anything that looked like shelter around here. He'd assumed that were-wolves needed a place out of the sun and wind to rest. Maybe he was wrong. More likely someone had access to teleportation magic. Depending on how powerful they were, they could be just about anywhere.

"Let's pack it in for now. This is a dead end and we've only got an hour of sunlight left anyway."

He was about to turn and fly away when something

caught his eye. A glint of metal maybe? Whatever it was, it was the first thing he'd seen of even remote interest.

He dropped toward the ground but didn't land. This could well be a trap and Daisuke had no interest in flying into it. What he found was a man half buried in the dirt. The flash came from a bracelet on his unburied wrist. The bracelet glowed in the ether but seemed harmless.

When nothing happened for five minutes, he wrapped the man in a bubble of ether and pulled him out of the earth. He wore only a tattered loincloth and had a deep, filthy wound in his side. A closer look revealed no sign of the werewolf curse. By some miracle he was still alive.

Though that would likely change if he didn't receive treatment soon. Carter was good at light magic, including healing.

Daisuke turned toward camp, carrying the unconscious Aborigine in the ethereal cocoon. Hopefully he didn't wake up halfway there and freak out. With that wound, it wouldn't take much to finish him off.

"Don't you think this is a little too convenient, Master?"

"Maybe, but if it's a trap, it the worst trap I've ever seen. There's no magical danger and if he's sick, we've got more than enough magic between us to deal with it before it becomes an issue. More likely he was part of the group that fled, but couldn't keep up with his wound so they abandoned him on the assumption that he'd die in short order. Why he didn't is another question altogether."

The sun had nearly set when Daisuke landed beside the parked dune buggy. Jinx appeared beside him as he gently lowed the wounded man to the ground and banished the cocoon. Helena and the others were sitting around the fire sipping something from steaming mugs.

Helena immediately leapt to her feet and hurried over. Carter and Justine approached more slowly.

"Where have you been?" Helena asked. "We were worried."

"Sorry about that. I found this unfortunate fellow half buried in the dirt and near death. He's not cursed. I was hoping Carter could put him back together again. Assuming he lives, maybe he can tell us something useful. Unless you guys found something, we're out of leads."

Carter knelt beside the injured man, his hands already glowing with healing energy. "All we found was another burned-out village. No survivors."

Daisuke grunted, disappointed but hardly surprised. "Please tell me we have something to eat. All that flying left me starving."

"We've got peanut butter, apples, ham, bread…" Justine trailed off.

"Perfect." Daisuke went to the larder and fixed himself two sandwiches with all that on them and stacked as high as he could fit in his mouth. He devoured the food in short order and downed a large glass of water. "Thanks."

"I've got him stabilized," Carter said. "But he really needs a hospital and an IV with fluids and minerals. A blood transfusion wouldn't hurt anything either."

"You can take him if you want to." Daisuke slumped beside the fire. "I'm done until morning."

"How far to the nearest hospital that could actually do the poor fellow any good?" Helena asked.

"About a thousand miles." Carter sat as well and shook his head. "I was pointing out his condition more than suggesting a course of action. My magic might not be perfect, but he should recover. Did you see anything that might hint at where the survivors went?"

"I didn't see a damn thing out in that wasteland. Best I can figure, they teleported somewhere. Though where that might be I can't begin to guess. I brought that guy in the hope that he could give us a clue. It's a thin hope, but all I've got."

Carter nodded. "Better than nothing. The healing magic will keep him docile until at least morning. I suggest we all get some sleep and start fresh tomorrow."

That struck Daisuke as a fine idea. He moved a few feet away from the fire, stretched out, and was soon fast asleep.

CHAPTER ELEVEN

A scream dragged Daisuke back to the land of the living. He sat up and looked around. There was no sign of battle. The man he'd rescued screamed again and flailed his arms and legs. With a little growl, Daisuke hit him with a paralysis spell, instantly rendering him still and silent.

A minute later everyone else came rushing out of their tents. Helena only had on an oversized t-shirt that left her legs mostly bare. Daisuke always liked that look.

Carter peered around with bleary eyes as if expecting to see an army of werewolves bearing down on them. "What?"

"Your patient woke up and decided the rest of us needed to join him. I paralyzed him."

"That's impossible. He shouldn't have woken until the healing spell finished closing his wound." Carter hurried over to the now-rigid Aborigine. "The wound is fully healed and only a small scar remains. That spell should've taken at least a full day to heal so much damage. He seems to be panicking. Release your spell, Daisuke. Justine, would you come here and translate for me?"

Daisuke snapped his fingers, sat up, and fumbled his phone out of his pocket. Barely midnight. No wonder his head felt like a watermelon that got stepped on by an elephant.

"Are you okay?" Jinx asked from behind him.

"Yeah, I guess. It's a good thing I got caught up on my sleep before we left for this mission." He stood just as Helena emerged from her tent for the second time, now wearing pants.

The three of them moved closer to Carter's group, but not so close that they'd startle the injured man.

Justine said something to him in his native tongue and got a hesitant reply. The conversation went back and forth a couple times before Justine finally said, "He's grateful for you rescuing him. I explained that he was safe in our camp. He's calmed down a little, but still seems jumpy."

"Who is he?" Carter asked.

Justine repeated the question. "His name is Bido and he's the son of the Jindo Tribe's shaman."

"See if he's willing to tell us his story."

Hesitantly at first then with growing strength Bido started to speak. Justine translated with a slight delay.

It all started six months ago during the Jindo's turn at protecting the holy artifact. Something happened to his father. An evil spirit twisted him up and turned him bad. He used strange magic to transform the people into monsters. With his new power, Bido's father conquered their former allies and made them into slaves. Only Bido was spared this fate.

His father had been contemplating expanding his

kingdom to more distant tribes when the man in white appeared and attacked. He struck the Arwa first. His father sensed it when the monsters he created died. He took Bido and his strongest followers into the wasteland to hide. Bido was a little too slow and got hurt by one of the enemy's beasts. The werewolves killed the beast that attacked him, but he was too hurt to keep moving. His father ordered him left behind.

"Ask him about the artifact," Carter said.

Daisuke listened closely, but had little doubt what Bido would say. Sure enough, Justine described the demon prison perfectly.

He moved a little ways away and ran a hand through his hair. This was so not good.

Helena joined him a moment later. "What do you think it means?"

"I wish I knew. Worst-case scenario, the prison has started to leak corruption. If it's bad enough, some of the demon's wickedness might be oozing out as well. I can't think of anything else that would explain what he just described."

"Is that even possible?"

"If it's not, then I don't know what the hell's going on. I need to talk to the boss. Maybe the Book of Wisdom mentions something like this." He turned to the others. "Carter, I'm borrowing your phone."

Carter waved but didn't move from his spot beside Bido.

Daisuke ducked into the tent and by the glow of a conjured light quickly found a large yellow satellite phone. He'd never used one before, but the keypad looked normal enough. He dialed, and after three rings the boss answered, "Carter?"

"No, boss, it's me. We've got a bit of a situation."

"A new situation?"

"Well, not exactly new. Sounds like the demon prison is leaking corruption and it's turned one of the local shamans evil. Looks like he's the source of the werewolves."

"You'd better tell me everything."

Daisuke did so. When he finished, he asked, "Does the book mention anything like this?"

"No and I've read it twice cover to cover. I suppose after thousands of years, even Solomon the Wise's magic would start to weaken. The problem is, if this is happening here, it might be happening everywhere. Heaven only knows what sort of chaos seventy-one leaking demon prisons might cause."

"I thought about that. The only positive I could think of was that this should make them easier to find. Of course, that applies to everyone looking for them, so that's not exactly ideal."

"You have a fine gift for understatement. Tell me more about the man in white."

Daisuke blinked, surprised at the sudden change of subject. "I don't know anything more. I only saw him from a distance. It looked like he opened a Heaven portal before he vanished into it. That's pretty rare. I don't even think Carter is strong enough to open one and he's our strongest divine magic user. Those white dogs were powerful enough to defeat werewolves, though it sounds like they're not invincible. Jinx says he's one of the people that killed her sisters. That's all I know. Is he someone familiar to you?"

"Not specifically, but I suspect you're dealing with priests rather than wizards. Only someone with a direct connection to one of the archangels could use a Heaven portal and command white wolves. Be very careful, Daisuke."

"I always am, boss. But shouldn't followers of the archangels be our allies?"

"You'd think so, but not every group is sufficiently open-minded. I mean, your familiar is a demon and you're working with a half demon. Those two facts by themselves are enough to make you all suspect in the minds of a fanatic."

"Great. So not only do I need to find a demon-possessed shaman and reclaim the prison, but I need to deal with a bunch of self-righteous angel worshippers at the same time. This job just keeps getting worse."

"At least you've got more help this time."

"There is that. Any thoughts on how I fix the prison?"

"Once you have the seal, it should be simple enough with the Staff of Law. Just find the gap in the ether and plug it."

"Gotcha, boss. I really hope it'll be as easy as you make it sound."

"It won't be, but I have great faith in you, Daisuke. Keep me informed."

She hung up, prompting him to shake his head. "Thanks, boss."

He tossed the phone on Carter's cot and ducked back out. Everyone had gathered around a freshly kindled fire. Bido appeared to have gone back to sleep, lucky devil.

"What'd she say?" Carter asked.

"The book says nothing about leaking prisons, but if I get the seal, I should be able to plug the leak. She also says that the man in white is more likely a priest than a wizard."

Carter's face scrunched up. "An archangel worshipper, all the way out here? I can't imagine what brought him to the middle of nowhere. There are large temples in the bigger cities, but we're generally not that devout as a people."

"Them," Jinx said. "There are at least three of them."

"Right," Carter said. "I didn't forget."

"Did your patient have any idea where his old man wandered off to?" Daisuke asked.

"Unfortunately not. According to Bido, there's nothing that way for days. If his father had a destination in mind, he didn't know what it might be."

"Sounds like we're stuck until your brother gets here." Daisuke lay back on his makeshift bed. "And if he doesn't know anything, I have no idea what our next move should be."

"Maybe if I show myself the man in white will come for me," Jinx said.

Daisuke rolled over to look at her. "You mean you'll act as bait? Not crazy about that plan."

"Neither am I, but isn't there a saying about desperate times?"

Daisuke grinned. "Yeah, but we're not that desperate yet."

CHAPTER TWELVE

Taking an entire day off given the current crisis seemed horribly wasteful to Daisuke, but with no real direction to focus his efforts, he had little choice. He did spend a few hours scrying using a basin of water as his vessel, but accomplished nothing for his efforts. After his initial outburst, Bido had been a calm and quiet presence in the camp, eating when given food but otherwise keeping to himself.

Having your father come under a demon's influence had to be a shock. Daisuke tried to imagine how he'd have felt if Yoshikazu had been in a similar state and failed to muster up much emotion. Had it been his mother, on the other hand, he would've happily murdered any demon that dared to try.

When the next day finally dawned, they were all eager to resume the hunt. Two hours after sunrise, a cloud of dust in the distance announced the arrival of something. Hopefully Carter's brother, but just to be safe, Daisuke said, "Take a look."

Ruq turned invisible and flew off. It took fifteen minutes,

but Ruq's telepathic voice said, *There are two trucks loaded with boxes. I sense four humans and nothing magical.*

That's great, come on back.

"We're good, it's just supply trucks."

"What did you think it was?" Carter asked.

"Given everything that's happened, I had no idea. My motto is, better safe than sorry."

"I thought your motto was blast them all and let the demon lords sort them out," Helena said.

"That's a good one too, but under different circumstances." Daisuke settled into his camp chair. "What's your brother like?"

"He's a nice guy." Carter sounded a little wistful. "Anson was always the good son. Worked hard, didn't get into trouble, took over the family business five years ago. Not a drop of magical ability in him."

"I can't picture you as a troublemaker," Helena said.

"A teenager with magical abilities is just asking for trouble. I grew out of pranks and tricks pretty quickly and never did anything very illegal."

"But slightly illegal?" Daisuke asked.

"When this is over I'll tell you about the time I snuck into the girls' locker room using an invisibility spell. It didn't end the way I'd hoped."

Daisuke could well imagine.

A few minutes later a pair of heavy-duty box trucks sporting upgraded suspensions and oversized tires came to a stop beside the camp. The driver's side door of the lead truck opened and an older version of Carter climbed down. Anson had started going gray at the temples and was dressed in khakis and work boots. He wore a broad-brimmed hat with one side bent vertical.

The brothers embraced and Carter led them back to Daisuke and the others. The three other people Ruq sensed got busy unloading heavy crates from the back of the first truck. Daisuke gave a silent command to his familiar to keep an eye on them.

You're getting paranoid.

Better than getting caught off guard.

"Everyone," Carter said. "I'd like you to meet my elder brother, Anson."

Anson waved. "G'day. Didn't reckon so many people would be here. No wonder you needed more supplies."

"We were hoping you could tell us more about who gave you that note," Carter said.

"Was there a problem?" Anson asked.

"I walked into a trap. All's well that ends well, but it could've been much worse." Beside Daisuke, Jinx winced as Carter glossed over her attack. "I figure whoever gave it to you is up to no good and I need to find them."

"Sorry, little brother. I never would've brought the bloody thing if I'd known. The lady didn't look like trouble. Fact is she had on a pin that marked her as an acolyte of the Binder's church. If you can't trust a nun in training, who can you trust?"

If the man in white was a priest, the Binder in Chains was the archangel most likely to cause trouble. Daisuke forced himself not to smile. Sounded like they had their next lead.

Carter gave his brother a pat on the back. "No worries, Anson. She might not have even known what was happening. If a higher-up said 'take this letter to Monk Deliveries,' she wouldn't have given it a thought."

"I reckon not. Still don't feel right walking my own blood into a trap. How long you staying out here anyway?"

"Till the job's done. Exactly how long that might be, I can't say. Back to the acolyte for a sec. Did you get her name?"

"'Fraid not, mate. The Warina church of the Binder isn't exactly a huge one. If they've got two nuns in training, I'll be shocked."

Carter nodded. "You heading back directly?"

"No, I've got three more stops this run. Why?"

"I was hoping we could get a ride in with you. I need to talk to this nun and find out what she knows."

"You can ride along if you want. We should be home by late afternoon. You can stay for supper, Mum would love that."

"I don't know if I have time," Carter said.

"Take the time," Daisuke said. "And be conspicuous. Take Justine and Helena with you. Act like nothing's wrong."

Carter nodded. "What about you?"

"Jinx and I will go ahead and get the lay of the land."

"While any interested eyes are looking at us. Not a bad plan." Turning to Anson, Carter asked, "Got room for three more?"

"Yeah, long as you don't mind riding in the back."

"Just like when we were kids."

"Hopefully we don't get in that much trouble."

The brothers laughed, but Daisuke seriously doubted that avoiding trouble was going to be possible.

Carter ended up riding in the cab of the lead truck with Anson while Helena and Justine rode in the back of the second. It wasn't that much more comfortable since none of the trucks had air-conditioning anyway. Bouncing along over the rough ground, heavy-duty shocks doing almost nothing to soften the ride; the whole thing brought back old memories. It also reminded Carter why he decided to leave home in the first place. He really wasn't cut out to be a delivery driver.

After ten minutes of silence Anson said, "So what the bloody hell's going on anyway?"

"You might be safer not knowing."

"That bad?"

"About as bad as it can get. Awful as things are, I'm happy the problems seem to be focused on the outback. If we had werewolves, demons, and heaven knows what else running around Sydney, I can't even imagine the body count."

"Werewolves? Really?" Anson's disbelief wasn't hard to understand. Even with everything Carter had seen around the world, this was the first time werewolves had shown up.

"Really." Carter blew out a long sigh. "You really want to know? Remember if I tell you, you can't share with anyone."

"I've never blabbed before, have I?"

Carter nodded and filled his brother in from the beginning. When he finished he added, "And that's how things stand. The surviving werewolves have disappeared, the ones hunting them have also vanished, and your mystery nun is my only lead. With any luck Daisuke will have things wrapped up with her by the time we get home."

"I don't know, mate. If that kid's a day over twenty, I'll eat my hat. You sure leaving it up to him's a good idea?"

"He's twenty-three and yes, I'm sure it's a good idea. Daisuke's our best field agent and he usually works alone. Running down leads like this is his specialty. We all do it, of course, but usually in teams of two or three."

Anson looked his way. "You were on this job alone."

"I did say usually. Plus, I'm the only member of the group that's an Australian citizen. The boss decided it was safest for me to go in on my own first. Soon as things got hairy, you'll notice, she sent backup."

"Yeah, I won't ask how you managed that little trick. There are some things I'm happier not knowing."

"It wasn't that hard to be honest. For a sealed country, we don't do an especially good job securing our borders."

"Don't let the pols hear you say that. Pretty sure there's a fine for it."

"Unlike the werewolves, that doesn't surprise me in the least. How are Mum and Dad?"

"Same as always. The old man retired in name only. He's still working in the garage from dawn to dusk. Mum keeps the house spotless and cooks too much. All very mundane and boring, especially to you, I expect."

"What do you say we start a new tradition and skip the argument this visit?"

"You only say that because you're going to lose." Anson grinned. "But what the hell. I'll let you off easy this time."

Carter smiled back. Despite everything, it was good to be home.

CHAPTER THIRTEEN

Daisuke decided to lounge around in camp for an hour after Carter and the others took off. He had no sense of being watched, but wanted to put on a good show just in case. With nothing better to do, he rummaged through the freshly arrived supplies and helped himself to some actual honeycomb. He gave a piece to Ruq before settling in a folding camp chair.

For his part, Bido seemed content to sit in the shade of the supply crates with his eyes closed. Leaving him alone in camp didn't seem like the best idea to Daisuke, but he wasn't sure what else to do with the man. As far as he could tell, everything that had happened left Bido in a sort of mental haze. It would be unsafe for him to just wander around the wastes alone. Well, Daisuke would think of something before they left.

Jinx sat on the ground using his blanket as a cushion. They had plenty of chairs, especially with just the two of them here, but she showed no interest in them. Instead, she fidgeted, first playing with her hair, then checking her nails, then back to the hair.

Finally unable to stand it he asked, "What's on your mind?"

"Why did you ask me to join you instead of Helena? You barely know me, but I assumed you two were close."

"We are close, reasonably anyway. Helena has a lot of wonderful qualities. Being sneaky isn't one of them. She is really good at creating barriers and bindings. I don't need either of those things on this part of the job. Whatever I might think of her personally, right now we have a task to complete and she's ill-suited to do it. You, on the other hand, are perfect. Your shadow magic lets you blend in and vanish at will. Your shadow webs are just as good for keeping a prisoner bound as any of Helena's spells. Finally, I think I've gotten a good sense of your personality over the last couple days and I trust you."

"I'm a half demon," she said. "Most humans distrust me on principle."

"Most humans are stupid or at least ignorant. They tend to judge people based on the shallowest, most irrelevant things. Skin color, wealth, manner of speech, ancestry—none of that matters on any deep level. Actions matter."

"Thank you." She started to wipe her eyes prompting him to look away. "Can I ask you something else?"

"Sure."

"Why do you wear those gloves?"

Daisuke tugged on the fingers of his right glove until it finally came off, revealing his burn scars. "Some people find these off-putting and I don't care much for being stared at. The gloves seemed a reasonable precaution."

Jinx winced. "They look painful."

"They were. Now they're just ugly." With nothing better to do he told her the story of how he got them. "After I failed the ritual, my family shipped me off to boarding school and I heard nary a word for ten years. Sorry as I am for the loss of your sisters, I can't help envying you the many years you had together."

"That might be the saddest story I've ever heard."

Daisuke chuckled and stood. "Then you need to hear more stories. I doubt mine's even in the top hundred. Let's get out of here. What did Anson say the name of that town was?"

"Warina." Jinx walked over, put a hand on his shoulder, and kissed his cheek. "Thanks for sharing part of your story."

"No big deal. Can you summon a shadow to keep an eye on Bido? He doesn't seem to be in any shape to get into trouble, but better safe than sorry."

"Sure." Ether swirled around Jinx and a moment later crimson eyes flashed in the shadow of Carter's tent. "There. My shadows are reasonably smart. If he tries anything, it'll drain just enough of his life force to render him unconscious without doing any permanent harm."

"Perfect, thanks."

Jinx vanished into his shadow and Daisuke took to the air. He'd have to think of some more stories to share later. That little kiss had sent a shiver down his spine.

Despite the lack of roads through the outback, it wasn't that hard to follow the delivery truck's path. The heavy loads had forced the tires to sink in about an inch, leaving a clear track. As soon as an actual road appeared, he cast an invisibility spell. Wizards weren't that uncommon here, but a Japanese guy flying over a sealed country would no doubt draw the attention of people he didn't want to deal with.

Another half an hour brought them within sight of a fair-sized town. Nothing outstanding by any means, but there were multiple streets, businesses, houses, a school, and three churches. That last seemed excessive given a population he guessed at no more than five thousand. Not that they were especially big churches. Each one had a bell tower and a chapel big enough for maybe two hundred people if they all took a deep breath.

After making his inspection flight, Daisuke landed in the shade of a palm tree at the edge of an empty playground and said, "Find the Binder's church."

For a change of pace Ruq didn't feel the need to grumble before flying away to search. Jinx appeared and leaned against the tree beside him. He forced himself to focus on their surroundings and not on her. A decidedly challenging task.

"Are you going to wait for the others to get here before you question the nun?"

"Not if I can catch her alone. I can't help thinking time isn't on our side."

"What if she calls for help?"

"Depends on how much help shows up. If it looks like I can't win, rest assured, I'm in no way averse to running away."

Found it, Master, but there's a problem.

What else is new? Lay it on me.

There's an anti-demon barrier on the church. I couldn't get inside.

That's not unusual for a church.

It is in this town. I checked all three and only the Binder's has such a barrier. What do you want me to do?

Keep you distance. I'm on my way.

"It seems the priests have taken extra precautions. There's an anti-demon barrier around the church. I'm not sure how it would affect a half demon, but I doubt it would be pleasant. You'll need to wait outside with Ruq."

"Going in alone might be risky."

"Everything in this business is a risk. This is a calculated one." Daisuke set out as soon as Jinx vanished into his shadow.

Following his connection to Ruq, he soon found himself standing across the street from a white-painted church with a steeple featuring a circle of chains front and center. The double doors were closed and no one was visible outside. It was midmorning on a weekday, so that didn't surprise him too much.

He glanced at the cafe across from him. A single young woman sat at one of the outside tables sipping what looked like iced tea, but otherwise there wasn't a soul in sight. It was actually a little creepy given the size of the town.

"I'm heading in," he whispered. "Can you jump to a different shadow?"

He watched his shadow stretch until it connected to the shadow between the cafe and the two-story apartment building beside it. No one else could see it thanks to the invisibility spell. When his shadow returned to normal, he strode across the street and up the steps to the front door.

After checking everything over through the ether, Daisuke was pretty sure there were no other protections beyond the demon barrier. The barrier itself was weird, different from any spell he'd ever seen. Maybe this was what a priest's magic looked like. He was only familiar with priests using healing magic.

Daisuke shrugged, let his invisibility spell fade, and

pushed the door open. He passed through a six-by-six vestibule and into the main chapel. Twenty rows of hard wooden benches faced an altar festooned with hanging chains. It reminded Daisuke of a torture chamber decoration rather than something holy.

To the right of the altar a door led into the private area of the church. A different spell glowed around that one, as best he could tell it was some sort of alarm. That made sense; you didn't want random people wandering into the priest's living space.

Now, how to go about getting someone's attention?

Knocking on the back door might do it, but it might also draw the attention of someone he'd prefer to avoid.

As he was debating his options, the back door opened and a young woman dressed in all black with a silver chain around her neck emerged. She smiled at Daisuke and hurried over. He smiled back, happy to play nice for the moment.

"Are you here to pray?" she asked.

"No, ma'am. I'm here to talk to you. I'm a friend of Carter Monk. He got the letter you asked his brother to deliver. I was hoping you could tell me how to find the X who signed it. There were a few issues in Milden Station and he asked me to look into them."

The nun's eyes got so wide that he could see the whites all the way around. She gave off a distinct scared-bunny vibe.

"Please don't run. My friend nearly got killed and I just want to know what's going on."

"I didn't know that was going to happen. Father Deal said it was for the greater good, that the Binder commanded it. It's not like I could refuse to deliver the letter."

"Of course you couldn't." Daisuke did his best to speak

slowly and softly. "An acolyte has to do as her superior commands. I know a little bit about your religion and obedience to superiors is an important part of it."

She took a couple deep breaths and seemed to calm down a fraction.

"Could we sit for a moment and talk?" he asked.

"I'll go make tea."

Before she could make a move Daisuke said, "I don't think that's a good idea. Let's just talk."

He guided her firmly but gently to the nearest bench and they sat.

"Why did Father Deal ask you to deliver that letter?"

"He said Carter Monk would know what to do when it arrived. That he'd help us complete our holy crusade."

"I see," Daisuke said, not really seeing at all. "I suppose if you did it to further the holy crusade, it's not so bad."

Her face lit up. "Exactly! It's so hard to live up to the Binder's example, but we're doing our best to complete the task he gave us."

"It is a challenge since we're only human. I'm a demon hunter myself, so I certainly understand the difficulties of dealing with immortal monsters. Would you tell me more about your crusade?"

Her cheeks flushed and she looked away, clearly embarrassed by his question. Why, he was less certain. "I only joined the church as a full nun this week, so I don't know all the details. Father Deal said our mission was to drive out all the unnatural creatures polluting our world."

"So he's a demon hunter as well?"

"Not just demons! All the unnatural creatures, demons, undead, spirits of all sorts. Anything that doesn't belong in the human realm must be either returned to where it came from or destroyed. It's the only way for humanity to truly thrive."

Daisuke nodded as if he believed this lunatic had a valid point. "A mission worthy of the Binder. I'd expect nothing less from the greatest of the archangels. Still, that's a titanic task for just the two of you."

"Oh no. Father Deal has three brothers helping him. When the time of their passing approaches, they'll each take an apprentice to assume their mission." Her face got even redder. "I... I hope that I can prove myself worthy enough to become Father Deal's apprentice one day."

"A laudable goal. Would it be possible for me to speak with Father Deal? As a demon hunter, I think there's plenty of room for us to cooperate. My work might be more specific, but it is essentially the same."

The nun finally looked up at him and offered her biggest smile yet. "Father Deal is at the Sanctuary with his brothers right now, but I'd be glad to pass him your message. I'm sure he'd welcome anyone willing to help complete the Binder's holy crusade."

Daisuke stood and held out his hand. "I'll stop by again tomorrow. Or better yet I can give you my cellphone number. Assuming I have a signal."

She grasped his hand and a tracking spell of Daisuke's own design attached itself to her. "Father Deal isn't fond of technology. He says it's a distraction from his work. Please stop by tomorrow after lunch. I'll have an answer for you by then, I'm certain."

Daisuke nodded. "I look forward to hearing good news."

He tried to let go but she refused. "I'm so rude. We didn't even exchange names. I'm Sister Eve."

"Daisuke. Pleasure to meet you."

"Likewise. See you tomorrow." She finally let go and hurried back the way she'd come.

Daisuke beat a hasty retreat as well. Assuming she had a magical way to contact Father Deal, he'd be able to listen in through the tracking spell. He didn't want to miss a word.

Father Deal paced and grumbled to himself as he considered his current conundrum. A group of were-wolves had escaped his efforts and even managed to kill one of his white wolves. That impressed and worried him in equal measure. Nothing less than a true demon should be strong enough to kill a beast summoned from Heaven itself. But he'd felt the beast die through their link and there was nothing else in the wasteland the tribes called home powerful enough to have hurt it.

He paused and turned toward the chain-draped altar at the rear of the Sanctuary. At least he and his brothers called it the Sanctuary. It was actually a temple to the Binder consecrated ages ago and forgotten about. One of his predecessors had found it and repurposed it to serve as the base of the League of Mortals.

Eliminating all immortal creatures in the world seemed like an impossible goal. In fact, many of those he'd approached over the years had laughed at him when he explained the group's mission. That had offended him when he was younger, but now he'd accepted that, by and large, humanity was too stupid to recognize what was good for it. Not that the bulk of the people would be of much use in dealing with the sorts of immortal dangers they faced on a regular basis.

He drew the sign of the chain, basically a horizontal figure eight, over his heart. Only the Binder's power allowed them to have a chance and he was most grateful for their patron's generosity.

A faint buzzing in the back of his mind drew Father Deal's attention to a silver mirror hanging behind the altar. His ever-loyal servant, Sister Eve, was trying to make contact. She had strict orders not to make contact unless it was an emergency and sufficient loyalty to obey those instructions.

The last thing he needed was more trouble. His brothers had left him to clean things up in Australia while they went to find the next target for their crusade. Finding the target wasn't the problem. They all knew where she was, it was a matter of figuring out how to get to her that was the trick.

At his mental command the ethereal link was completed and Sister Eve's ecstatic, slightly disconcerting face appeared in the mirror. She was even more flushed than usual today which was seldom a good sign.

"Sister, what has happened?"

"A potential ally has approached me, Father Deal. A demon hunter that seems willing to help with the holy crusade, at least to help with the demon part of it."

Deal kept his expression smooth, but inside his mind raced. No one ever approached them, it was always the other way around and then only after careful study. In fact, no one should even know they existed or were associated with the Binder's church.

"Tell me everything, Sister. A new ally could only increase our chances of success."

Her smile widened. "Exactly my thinking, Father."

She went on to tell him what she discussed with the

demon hunter. That he was a friend of Carter Monk's immediately put Deal on alert. Carter worked for a particular organization that would in no way be eager to team up with his. That was the main reason Deal had been willing to use him as a sacrifice to kill or at least hopefully weaken the half-demon witch. That plan had been a total waste of effort, but he'd assumed that it hadn't cost them anything.

It seemed he might've been wrong about that.

"And you say the demon hunter is coming back tomorrow after lunch to get my answer?"

"Yes, Father. Will you speak with him?"

"It would be rude if I didn't. What was his name?"

"Daisuke. Japanese I believe, probably from Cairns. They have a large Japanese population that immigrated before the borders were closed."

He nodded. Deal knew that name. Daisuke Kugo was another member of the same organization Carter belonged to and he was no more from Cairns than Deal was from Tokyo. "I'll remember that. You did well to contact me so quickly, Sister. Should he visit the church again, be sure to show him every hospitality."

"Of course, Father. I look forward to seeing you in person tomorrow."

He waved a hand, severing the connection. The meeting would be tonight and Deal's white wolves would make short work of Daisuke and anyone else that might interfere with his plans.

CHAPTER FOURTEEN

Daisuke sipped a cup of hot chocolate and frowned as he thought over everything Sister Eve and her superior, Father Deal, had said. The good father claimed he'd be there tomorrow after lunch, but Daisuke had serious doubts. Deal had to know that Daisuke wasn't friendly after what had been done to Carter. The idea that he might show up for a face-to-face meeting under those circumstances was ludicrous.

Of course that begged the question of what he did intend and unfortunately Daisuke had no real idea about that.

"You're deep in thought again," Jinx said.

They were seated across from each other at the little cafe near the church. He'd considered finding somewhere more private, but now that he'd made his play, hiding was a waste of time. Deal would do whatever he was going to and Daisuke would have to handle it when it happened.

"Sorry about that. Here I am on a date with a beautiful woman and I'm not even paying any attention to her.

Though I'm certainly the only one not paying any attention to you."

Both the sole other customer and the young woman that took their order stared at Jinx with obvious disbelief. Whether that was for her looks in general or the fact that her dress somehow defied gravity and kept her covered, Daisuke didn't know. Though he could certainly relate.

Jinx sipped her own tea and nibbled on a cookie. "It's a little uncomfortable, but I sense no malice in their looks."

"No, if there's anything to sense, I suspect it would be envy." Daisuke grabbed a cookie—oatmeal raisin, not his favorite, but after no sweets for three days, far better than nothing—and held it under the table for an invisible Ruq. "I further suspect you're the most beautiful woman to ever set foot in this town if not on the continent."

She smiled. "It's the magic. Mom was pretty, but my sisters and I have always been something extra. Human and demon must be a good combination."

Jinx didn't say it with any sort of excess pride, rather as a simple statement of fact.

"I've met other half demons, and I can assure you, none of them even came close to you. But to be fair, they were both male and trying to kill me, so they may have just not been to my taste."

"And I am?"

Daisuke grinned. "Oh, yes."

Her cheeks reddened, giving her an almost innocent expression that combined with the decidedly naughty rest of her to produce a warm feeling in him, only not in his cheeks. If only he wasn't on a job in the middle of nowhere. He hadn't seen so much as a hotel.

As noon approached, the cafe got busier, so Daisuke

decided they needed to take their leave. He was pumped with sugar and ready for a walk anyway. He paid the bill and left a nice tip then they set out.

Instead of hiding in his shadow, Jinx walked beside him, holding his arm. With no destination in mind, Daisuke just wandered the streets. They passed a general store, a diner, and a laundromat along with many houses and apartment buildings. Eventually they reached the business district, which was really just the edge of town. He counted a dozen warehouses, a slaughterhouse reeking of blood, and a mechanic shop. Weary, dusty men stopped in their tracks as he passed. Or more accurately, as Jinx passed.

Not one spoke to them. They just stared, mouths slightly open.

"If I ever need to shoplift," Daisuke said. "I'm going to have you come with me and chat with the clerk. I could walk out with the whole store and no one would even notice."

"I may need to get different clothes when our business is finished. The shadow silk is nice when I'm expecting trouble, but it is a little revealing."

"If you're in Zurich this winter, it'll also be chilly. Does cold bother you? I know some people with demon blood are resistant to extremes in temperature."

"The cold won't hurt me, but I don't find it comfortable either. A light jacket along with my natural immunity is enough."

They found their way back to the empty park and settled on the swing set. Time passed quickly with idle chatter until his phone rang. "Helena?"

"We're back. The Monk family business is at the edge of town. We're eager to hear how things went."

"We passed the place on our scouting run earlier. See you in a minute." He hung up.

"Scouting run? Not the most romantic name for our first date."

"True, but it did make it sound more like work so at least I won't get a lecture for enjoying myself while she was gone. And it was a scouting run. I'm pretty comfortable with the lay of the land now. Come on."

They left the park and made their way back to the business district. Jinx didn't hold his arm this time which was a disappointment, but probably wise all the same. They found Carter waiting outside a fenced-in compound with a sign that read, "Monk's Deliveries."

"How'd it go?" Daisuke asked.

"No issues, though I was reminded how boring the family business is. Helena filled in the hole she left in the middle of Milden Station's main street. The locals were trying to do it with shovels and had made pretty good progress. No one complained when she finished up for them."

"I bet not." They fell in behind Carter, who led them to a smaller building beside the sprawling main warehouse. "Do you want Justine to hear what I have to say?"

"Is it bad?"

"Bad enough. Looks like the man in white is a member of another crazy magical cult. I admit that I've run into enough of them now that it doesn't bother me much. For someone not part of this world, finding out your local priest of the Binder is a member of a cult in addition to his actual faith might be a bit hard to take."

"She's in this up to her neck. I'll give her the choice. If she wants to listen, fine. If not, also fine."

Daisuke shrugged, not caring either way. Carter was the

senior man on this mission, so it was his call. If the boss didn't like it, he'd be the one catching hell.

When they reached the door Carter opened it and motioned Daisuke and Jinx inside before closing it behind him. A potent ward settled over the building courtesy of Helena, who was sitting at a round table beside Justine. Workbenches covered with tools and parts ran along three walls and the smell of grease, oil, and diesel covered everything. Not the nicest place for a planning session, but out here you had to take what you could get.

Daisuke sat beside Helena with Jinx on his right while Carter took the last chair beside Justine.

"Go ahead and make your report, Daisuke," Carter said.

He did so, relaying everything he'd learned from talking to Sister Eve then later spying on her. All he left out was his date with Jinx. That had no bearing on the mission and would only lead to a discussion he wasn't ready to have.

When Daisuke finished Helena said, "That's insane. Demons I could understand. No offense, Jinx."

"What about me?" Ruq demanded. "Your anti-demon bias is most upsetting."

Helena ignored the imp's outburst. She'd heard enough of them after all. Ruq huffed, shimmered into view in rat form, and settled on Daisuke's lap. A few pats on the back seemed to soothe his bruised ego.

"As I was saying," Helena continued. "Angels are a net good for the world and elemental spirits are a natural part of it. Who knows what getting rid of the latter will do to the ecosystem?"

Daisuke wasn't sure if he should point this out or not, but she was mistaken about one thing. "Actually, elemental spirits aren't a natural part of the world. There used to be no spirits here, but when the four elemental kings made deals with human wizards, they sent many spirits through to our world to serve their new human allies. A few more slipped through every time a portal was opened until eventually they were everywhere."

"I never knew that," Helena said.

"Neither did I," Carter added. "Are you sure?"

"It's what I was taught as a kid. After all, the first member of the Kugo clan made a bargain with the King of Fire and the other master clans made deals with the other elemental lords. I suppose it might be propaganda—nothing the master clans did would surprise me at this point—but I can't see why they'd bother."

"Does it really matter?" Justine asked. When everyone looked at her she hastened to add, "I just mean for our current situation. I'm sure it matters in the grand scheme of things."

"I'm not sure it matters in the grand scheme either," Daisuke said. "Things are the way they are and four overly ambitious priests aren't going to change that. All we need to focus on now is capturing Deal alive so we can force him to tell us where the boss's friend is."

"I can handle that," Helena and Jinx said at the same time.

The two women glared at each other like a pair of angry cats. Only the hissing was absent.

"Maybe you could work together," Carter said.

The pair turned their angry stares on him forcing Daisuke to suppress a smile. Sticking your nose into a fight between women was never a good idea.

Bless his heart, Carter soldiered on. "Shadow webs plus a binding spell would be sure to render him incapable of fighting back."

"I don't need her help!" Both women spoke in unison once again.

It was becoming a comedy routine now and Daisuke struggled to hold in his laughter. It was an absurd reaction considering what they were dealing with, but he couldn't help it. The tension of the last couple days had built to the point that it needed a release somewhere. And since sex was off the table, that left laughing or blowing something up.

"Just think about it," Carter said. "We've got until tomorrow afternoon to come up with a real plan. For tonight, let's just get rested up and ready for morning. My parents invited us to join them for dinner and I'll have you know my Mum is a great cook."

"I've never turned down a home-cooked meal," Daisuke said. "Please tell me we're having crocodile."

"We are not having crocodile. We're having steak."

"Kangaroo steak?" Daisuke asked, mostly in the hope of getting a reaction.

"No, beef. We have cows in Australia, I'll have you know."

"You're shattering all my illusions, Carter."

Helena snickered and it was like a dam broke. Soon they were all howling with laughter. Except Jinx, but she did chuckle. Perhaps the humor eluded her. To be fair, it wasn't all that funny anyway.

When they could all breathe again Carter said, "Anyone that wants to use the shower in the guest room is welcome. Dinner's at seven."

A hot shower and a home-cooked meal. Daisuke's night was looking up.

CHAPTER FIFTEEN

For all his joking, Daisuke had seldom enjoyed a more pleasant meal. The simple, hearty food had warmed him body and soul. And the scrumptious apple cobbler with ice cream had left him wanting way more. Forced to remain invisible, Ruq had demanded leftovers, but Daisuke wasn't sure there'd be any for him to share.

When the meal was over Daisuke sighed and pushed back from the long table where his group sat with the Monk clan including Carter's parents, Anson, his wife, and their two sons. The boys were both in their early teens and couldn't stop staring at Jinx. Having once been thirteen, he knew exactly how they felt. Helena got her share of looks as well, which would hopefully improve her mood.

"Absolutely delicious, Mrs. Monk," Daisuke said. "I can't tell you how wonderful a meal like this is on a mission."

"Aw, save your flattery. This is the least we could do for a friend of Carter's."

"The least *I* can do is the dishes." When she started to

object Daisuke shook his head. "I insist. Enjoy some time with your family."

Daisuke started collecting plates and Helena stood to help. Jinx stayed seated. Maybe her shadows usually handled the housework. Or cavework since that was where she lived. A couple invisible hand spells allowed him to carry everything Helena couldn't handle in one trip.

The kitchen was pretty basic, but it had a sink and a washcloth, which was all he needed. Not that he actually planned to wash the dishes himself.

They piled everything in the sink and Helena said, "How come you never offer to do the dishes at your apartment?"

"We never have any dishes at my apartment, we always get takeout."

"I could cook, assuming you even want me to visit anymore."

"Why wouldn't I want you to visit anymore?" He summoned a pair of invisible spirits who got busy washing and stacking up the dishes.

"You're clearly into Jinx. Not that I can blame you."

"I do like her, I won't deny that. But I didn't suddenly stop liking you. I've known her for a couple days. We're not looking to get married tomorrow. You and I have been friends for, what, four years now? Whatever happens between me and Jinx, I see no reason for us to stop being friends."

"Is that all we are?" Helena asked.

"Is that not enough?" Daisuke countered.

"I never really thought that much about it until I saw you and Jinx together. The jealousy hit me hard."

"Once again the boss's powers of observation prove greater than my own."

"What do you mean?"

"I was flirting with her after I got back from Japan and she said I'd better not let you see me doing that. I told her you weren't the jealous type. Shows what I know." Daisuke took a step closer and put his arm around her. "We'll figure it out when we get back, all three of us."

"I don't know what that dirty mind of yours is conjuring up, but I'm not into that sort of thing."

Daisuke kissed her forehead. "That's not what I was suggesting. Though now that you mention it, I can't figure out why I wasn't suggesting it."

She punched him on the shoulder. "You—"

They both went still when a tremor ran through the ether. Someone had just cast a powerful spell.

Daisuke ended his spell, leaving the dishes half washed in the sink, and hurried back into the dining room with Helena. Carter and Jinx were on their feet, tense, and looking around as if expecting a demon to appear at any moment.

"You felt it?" Helena asked.

Carter nodded. "Outside the compound I'd say, but still close."

"What's going on?" Anson asked.

"We've attracted some unwelcome attention." Carter moved around the table and helped his mother up. "You guys need to get somewhere safe. Whatever's coming, it'll be after us. We'll do our best to draw them away from the house."

"We can use the pantry," Carter's father said. "Come on, everyone."

"Helena?" Carter asked.

"I'll seal the door and make sure no one gets in."

"Four white wolves are approaching fast," Jinx said. "They already destroyed three of my shadows."

"If the white wolves are here then Deal is as well," Daisuke said. "Carter, if you and Jinx can handle the wolves, I'm going for Deal."

"No!" Jinx said at once. "We don't dare divide our forces any further. The wolves are too strong."

As the only member of the group that had actually fought them, Jinx certainly knew more about what they were dealing with than Daisuke did.

"Alright, we stick together. Ruq, find Deal, but keep well away." He sensed his familiar's acknowledgement.

Daisuke was about to ask about strategy when the front door exploded inward. A white wolf as tall as Daisuke's shoulder shook wood chips out of its fur and bared its fangs. Three stepped into the dining room and they fanned out facing Daisuke and his companions. The wolves fairly crackled with divine energy. So much so that he was pretty sure they were summoned directly from Heaven. Angelic wolves didn't seem like they should be a thing, but clearly they were.

The largest wolf's muscles tensed.

Before it could jump, Daisuke hit it full in the chest with a blast of black lightning.

The attack blew it back out the hole it just made.

The spell wasn't enough to kill it, unfortunately, which gave Daisuke a rough idea of the sort of power he was dealing with.

Snarling, the remaining three wolves leapt.

Carter summoned a shield of white light that turned two of them aside and Jinx blasted the third with an inky-black lance of energy, drawing a pained yelp as it staggered and fell partway to the floor.

Not one to waste an opening, Daisuke conjured a black

disk under the wounded wolf and finished it with a column of black lightning. Rather than leaving a corpse, the wolf turned into a ball of light that vanished in a burst of sparkles.

That confirmed these were summoned monsters at least. Conjuring something this strong had to take a toll on Deal. If they could defeat the wolves, the priest should be easy to capture.

Daisuke smiled to himself and blasted another wolf in the face just as it broke through Carter's shield. His spell burned half its muzzle off, but didn't slow it much.

Clearly, dealing with the wolves would be easier said than done.

Shadows appeared from nowhere, attacking the uninjured wolf from every direction. It snapped at them, destroying one with every bite. The shadows' claws must have been doing something though, as the wolf continued to slow.

Daisuke summoned another black disk under it and finished it off.

A scream from the kitchen distracted him, but Carter cut off the final wolf before it could capitalize on his inattention. "We're good here. Go!"

Daisuke didn't need to be told twice.

He rushed through the kitchen door to find the first wolf he blasted clawing and biting at Helena's barrier. The golden dome was looking pretty ragged.

Daisuke's eyes burned as he summoned Crimson Haze.

You wouldn't think something that looked like a wolf could scream like a hurt child, but you'd be wrong. If it was an attempt to manipulate the emotions of the one it was fighting, the beast was wasting its time. Once Daisuke decided someone or something was his enemy, nothing would stop him from putting an end to it. Especially if it was threatening someone he cared about.

Fifteen seconds under the effects of Crimson Haze put the wolf on its belly and turned its screams to whimpers.

The stinging in Daisuke's eyes grew worse by the moment, but finally the wolf exploded in a burst of golden motes.

He fell to his knees and blew out a breath. By heaven he hated holding the spell for that long.

Before he knew it Helena was at his side. "Are you okay?"

"Yeah, no sweat. How about you?"

Her answer came in the form of a long kiss. As thank-yous went it was one of the better ones he'd gotten. The silence from the dining room led him to believe the battle was over.

Ruq. Did you find him?

Yes, Master. The priest is on his way to his church. Very slowly, I might add. Doesn't look like he has much fight left in him.

Good. Stay on his tail. We'll be there as soon as we can.

Helena pulled away and glared at him. "Were you talking to Ruq while I was kissing you?"

"Yes. Please don't take it personally. Your kiss was excellent, but we're still in the middle of something here."

Daisuke forced himself to his feet and went out into the dining room. All the furniture had been smashed to bits, there were burn marks all over the place, and the less said about the hole in the front of the house the better.

"Your parents have insurance, right?" Daisuke asked.

"Yes, but I doubt this is covered. Did you find Deal?"

"Ruq's on his trail and it looks like he's heading for the church. I suggest we get after him and that your family remains inside Helena's barrier until he's wrapped up."

"No argument," Carter said.

The group hurried out with Carter in the lead. Since he grew up here he certainly knew the area better than any of them.

"Are you okay?" Jinx asked.

"Yeah, why?" She touched Daisuke's face and showed him her bloody finger. "Oh, well, that's an unfortunate side effect of the spell I used to kill the final wolf. No big deal, assuming I don't have to use it again anytime soon."

"And if you do?"

"Then I'll deal with it. Don't worry."

From her expression, he doubted Jinx would be able to do as he asked, but at least she didn't feel compelled to say anything else on the subject. There really was nothing to be done about it. He never used Crimson Haze unless he had to. Or his temper got the better of him. Since none of his family was here, he doubted the latter would happen.

A block from the church Ruq landed on his shoulder, now looking like an owl. "The priest went in about a minute ago. I sensed no magic, so he should still be in there."

"Good work."

"Good enough to get me some of that dessert?"

"The cobbler's all gone, but if you promise not to make a mess, I might be persuaded to find you some ice cream."

"Disappointing, but I'll take it."

The group stopped across the street from the church. There were no streetlights, but a powerful floodlight over the door lit up the nearby area. Not that there was anything to see. Warina had little in the way of nightlife.

"How do you want to handle this?" Daisuke asked.

"We need Deal alive, otherwise I'd say we blow up the church and have it over with." Carter scratched his chin then closed his eyes. "I sense two people, Deal and the nun most likely. The direct way is likely the best. I'll take point."

Carter sprinted across the street and stopped outside the door. He closed his eyes again. "No traps that I can sense."

"I'll wait out here to make sure he doesn't escape," Jinx said.

The anti-demon barrier made that a necessity, but Daisuke appreciated her offering all the same. "Ruq, you'll be keeping the lady company."

The imp hopped from his shoulder to Jinx's.

Daisuke nodded and Carter tapped the door.

It exploded inward and they followed a moment later.

Just in front of the chain-festooned altar stood Sister Eve. She raised her hands out to the side. "How dare you enter this holy place with violence? You all need to leave."

Daisuke stepped around Carter. "Your boss decided to pay us an early visit and he wasn't terribly polite. When someone tries to kill me, I take it personally. When they try and kill people I care about, I get angry. As a famous character once said, you won't like me when I'm angry. Now, you can take us to Deal or we can tear this church apart looking for him. Your choice."

She frowned and lowered her arms with a sigh. "You seemed nicer the last time you visited."

"Did you miss the part where I said Father Deal tried to kill us?"

"If he did, you must be consorting with unnatural creatures. Are you really a demon hunter?"

"Yes. No more stalling. Where is he?"

She shook her head and remained silent.

"Have it your way."

He grabbed her forehead and sent a tiny bolt of black lightning into her brain. After a single shudder she collapsed.

Everyone was staring at him. "What? We can't have her sneaking up behind us and I only used enough juice to knock her out for a few hours. Or days. Either way she'll be fine."

He strode toward the door that led to the living area. A wave of his hand dispelled the ward and sent chunks of wood flying into the hall beyond the entrance.

No sign of Deal, but there were three more doors to check.

Carter grabbed his arm and pointed at the nearest door to the left.

Daisuke nodded, eased closer, and drew a symbol on the door.

Carter darted past him and took up position on the far side.

When Helena touched his shoulder, Daisuke triggered the spell.

The door disintegrated and he leapt through.

No magic assaulted him and no monsters tried to tear him apart. Deal lay on the room's sole bed in a puddle of his blood. A kitchen knife made it clear that he'd cut his own throat.

Carter raised his glowing hands and pressed them over the still-spurting wound. "You're not getting out of it that easily, damn you."

Daisuke usually had great faith in Carter's healing abilities, but there was an awful lot of blood on the mattress. While Carter did his work, Daisuke put a finger on Deal's forehead and concentrated. As he'd told Ruq earlier, mind reading wasn't an exact science, but he needed to figure out where Deal came from and how to get there.

The first memory he found was of an ancient temple to the Binder. The priests came and went via magic.

He went further back.

The images were starting to dim. It seemed Carter was losing his battle.

"Come on," Daisuke muttered as he sifted through endless images of battles with all manner of magical creatures. "You didn't get there by portal the first time. Where is it?"

The memory was so dark he could barely make out any details. There was a huge mountain thrusting up seemingly in the middle of nowhere. Deal was at the base when a door burst into glowing life and he passed through it.

The image had nearly faded to nothing when Daisuke yanked his finger away. That had been far too close. Being stuck in someone's mind when they died was not an experience he recommended. He'd done it once and hoped to never do so again.

"I couldn't save him." Carter's hands were soaked with blood and he actually looked upset about his failure.

"Not exactly a huge loss to humanity," Daisuke said. "I've got a rough idea where their base is, but finding it might be a trick. What do you want to do with this mess?"

"Leave it," Carter said. "The police will clean up everything tomorrow."

"You sure?" Daisuke asked. "Sister Eve is certainly going to tell them we killed Deal. I can disintegrate his body and we can torch the church to cover our tracks."

"We can't just burn down a church," Helena said.

Daisuke cocked his head. "Why?"

"What do you mean, why? It's a church. It would be disrespectful."

"Seriously? The priest that runs the place tried to kill us. I call that disrespectful."

"The chief constable isn't an idiot," Carter said. "One look at this scene and he'll know Deal killed himself. The partially healed wound will prove we tried to save him. I can't see that there'll be any problems. Especially since we'll be long gone by the time he arrives."

It was Carter's call and if that's how he wanted to play it, Daisuke was content to follow his lead.

CHAPTER SIXTEEN

Daisuke felt a little bit bad about leaving the Monk house at first light instead of offering to help fix the damage caused by Deal's white wolves. Tracking down the hidden temple was more important and Anson had assured them that no one blamed them for what happened. A kind sentiment, but bullshit. Their presence had been if not directly then at least indirectly responsible. Justine had offered to stay behind and help clean up at least. He appreciated that mainly because it saved him the trouble of asking her to stay.

"How far do we have to go?" Carter asked. He and Helena were flying on his conjured light board while Daisuke flew with Jinx in his shadow.

"About a thousand miles. Assuming the mountain I found on my search is the same one that I saw in Deal's memories. We won't know for sure until we get there."

"That's at least five hours," Carter said. "No way can I maintain this spell for so long, especially if we have to fight after we arrive."

"I suggest we stop and rest at hour four. Then hit the mountain after lunch."

Helena shook her head. "How can you make this sound like an afternoon outing? There might be three more priests and who knows how many white wolves waiting for us."

"I don't think so," Daisuke said. "Deal's memories were pretty hazy, but it looked to me like his buddies were off scouting their next target. He didn't seem to know exactly where they were, but it wasn't the temple. If it makes you feel better, I can try and act more nervous."

Helena took her right hand off Carter's waist and shot Daisuke a middle finger. He grinned back. Angry Helena was more useful than nervous Helena. And if it did come to a fight, she and Jinx would be the only ones at full strength. They'd have to carry the weight this time.

Daisuke was running on fumes when they finally spotted a lake surrounded by palm trees that looked like a good resting spot. A few crocodiles were sunning themselves on the bank, but after everything they'd been through the huge reptiles didn't overly worry him.

They landed a safe distance away and settled in the shade of some of the palm trees. Jinx appeared from his shadow and sat to his left. She gave him a worried look. "You look beat."

"I can find no fault with your assessment."

Helena shrugged off the backpack Anson's wife had given her and handed out homemade lunches wrapped in tinfoil. Handmade by Mrs. Monk, not Helena, which meant the food should be delicious.

Jinx accepted hers, waited for Helena to turn around, and handed the packet to Daisuke. "I ate last night, so I'm good for another week."

"Thanks."

He dug into his sandwich first. The roast beef was delicious, just as expected. There was even a little bag of cookies in the bottom. He offered them to Ruq but the imp refused.

"You need all the strength you can get. While I enjoy the sweets, I don't actually need to eat, unlike you."

That might be the most thoughtful thing his familiar had ever said.

"If you die I go back to hell where an angry demon lord is waiting for me."

"That's more like it."

Jinx laughed. "You two are adorable."

Daisuke snapped his fingers. "Speaking of familiars, how's Bido doing? You can check through your shadows, right?"

"I peek in on him every couple hours. He mostly eats and sleeps. I feared he might try and run away, but he seems content in our camp."

"Probably the lack of werewolves makes it appealing. When we wrap this end up, I can use him to find his father and the demon prison, so I'm glad he hasn't wandered off."

"How?"

Daisuke broke into the second lunch and found a carbon copy of the first. Given the quality of the first helping, that suited him fine.

"Blood magic. The family bond between parent and child is strong enough to act as a link."

"I'm not familiar with that school of magic." Jinx leaned back against the tree.

"It's a branch of necromancy. I didn't study it that closely since it's not very useful against demons. They don't have what you'd consider actual blood. Or at least what the spell considers blood." He finished off the last of the cookies and sighed. "I feel so much better."

"You still need to rest." Jinx patted her lap. "Why don't you lie down?"

That sounded like an excellent idea. It also sounded like an idea liable to get him yelled at later. He leaned back, settled his head on her soft thighs, and sighed again. Totally worth it.

He closed his eyes. Actual sleep seemed unlikely, but he could certainly rest.

When he opened his eyes again the shadows had lengthened considerably. Had he actually fallen asleep? Must've been more tired than he thought.

He looked up at Jinx who smiled down at him. "Sleep well?"

"Yeah, thanks to the pillow. Did your legs fall asleep?"

"No. We half demons are made of sturdier stuff. You could sleep on my legs all day and I'd never notice."

"Now there's an ideal way to spend a day."

"If you two are done flirting," Helena said. "We need to get going."

Daisuke grinned and sat up. She couldn't have been too upset if she didn't wake him up and demand he move.

Forty-five minutes later they spotted the mountain jutting up out of the desert. The article he'd read said it was called the Mystery Mountain because it just appeared out of nowhere one day, no warning, no earthquake, just poof, here's an entire mountain in the middle of the desert. Weird as it was, magic was a thing and no one got overly worked up about it. The authorities investigated, found nothing dangerous or remarkable, other than its location of course, shrugged, and went on about life.

The temple must have been built later since there was no mention of anything magical at the site. They landed at the base of the mountain and Daisuke blew out a breath. Thank goodness for the extra lunch and nap. He was a bit tired, but nowhere near reaching backlash. He offered a silent prayer to any archangel other than the Binder that they found the temple free of priests and monsters. If Xerxes happened to be here, so much the better.

Jinx appeared beside him an instant before Carter said, "Helena, you're up."

As an expert in barrier and binding magic, Helena would have the easiest time finding the entrance. It would also give Daisuke and Carter another chance to rest, which he wouldn't turn down.

"Should I help?" Jinx asked.

Daisuke shook his head. "Helena's good at this sort of thing. Save your strength in case we need to fight."

They both turned to watch Helena walk around the base of the mountain. It looked kind of like a child's drawing of a mountain—a cone jutting up out of flat ground. It wasn't a perfect cone of course. There were three jagged peaks and the base was oval and irregular. Daisuke tried to imagine how much power it would take to plop a mountain down in the middle of the desert and failed.

It wasn't so much that the process would be complicated. First you'd have to go to the plane of earth and slice one of the mountains there off at the base, then open a portal big enough for it to fall through. Only an archangel or demon lord would have the raw power needed to do something like that. And, since there was a temple of the Binder inside, he had a pretty good idea which one was responsible.

"Found it," Helena said. "The barrier's pretty strong and

I've never seen an illusion quite like this. I can't dispel it on my own."

Daisuke, Jinx, and Carter walked over to where Helena stood in front of a section of mountain that looked pretty much the same as every other section. Even peering through the ether there was nothing to distinguish it. That's what made high-level illusions so tricky. They blended in both in the real world and in the ether. He had no idea what Helena saw that tipped her off, but he was certain she knew what she was talking about.

"I can crack the illusion," she said. "It's the barrier beyond that's the problem."

Helena raised both hands and a spike of ether formed. It shot out, slammed into the mountain, and transformed into a wedge that slowly spread the stone open. Since stone didn't bend, Daisuke finally knew where the illusion was. Eventually both the illusion and the wedge shattered into motes of ether.

Beyond the illusion was a carved entrance of smooth white stone. Pillars carved to resemble winged men wrapped with chains held up a stone roof. Under the roof was a twelve-foot-tall set of double doors.

"Are they expecting giants for dinner?" Daisuke asked.

"The entrance is meant to foster awe," Carter said. "And I see what you meant about the barrier, Helena. It's quite dense."

Daisuke shook off his annoyance at the pompous doorway and focused. Without the illusion obscuring it, he had no trouble reading the ether. The barrier combined anti-demon magic with a purely physical wall. Not especially complex magic, but the amount of power behind it was an issue.

He grabbed a handy rock and chucked it with all his might at the temple. The barrier flared as soon as the rock hit and in a flash all that remained was dust. So he'd been wrong. It was a disintegration barrier rather than a simple wall. That was much worse.

"I'm afraid we're just going to have to overwhelm it," Daisuke said.

"What did you have in mind?" Carter asked.

"I say we blast chunks of rock out of the mountain above the door and let them rain down until the barrier gives out. That should drain us less than any other option."

No one objected so they all started firing off their most destructive spells. Boulders of varying sizes rained down only to get reduced to dust. Finally, Daisuke carved one out the size of a modest sedan and let it fall. Half of it vanished before the barrier finally shattered and the rest landed with a thud in front of the door.

"That could've been worse," Daisuke said. "Looks like the anti-demon barrier was tied to the disintegration barrier. They're both gone now."

"Lucky me," Ruq muttered.

Daisuke led the way around the boulder he'd dropped and up the stairs toward the huge doors. He eyed the statues, but they didn't come to life and try and smash them flat as they passed. Seemed excessive for decorations, but after summoning the mountain, carving a few statues would be a piece of cake.

A light shove was enough to get the doors to swing silently open, revealing a long, empty corridor. It ran without a twist or turn to another pair of equally large doors. There were no side passages or other doors, so that at least made the decision about which way to search first easy.

"I'll go first," Helena said. "If there's anything hidden, I'll be most likely to spot it."

Daisuke stepped aside to let her take the lead. Some might say that wasn't very chivalrous, but he knew what Helena could do and her assessment of the situation was correct. Daisuke's ego wasn't so bloated that he failed to see that.

Not that it mattered in the end. The group reached the next door without issue and this time Helena pushed it open. Inside was a massive altar chamber with a domed ceiling so high Daisuke couldn't see the top. He wouldn't have been surprised if it ran all the way to the peak of the mountain.

"Heaven's mercy," Helena said.

Daisuke dragged his gaze away from the ceiling to see what bothered her so much. It didn't take long to figure it out. Above the chain-draped altar, someone had crucified an angel. The unconscious angel wore only a wrap that covered him from waist to midthigh. Daisuke was thoroughly into women, but even he could admit that this was the most beautiful man he'd ever seen.

Black iron nails bigger than railroad spikes had been driven through the angel's hands, feet, and wings. Blood had run down the white wall, staining it red. A small trickle still leaked out of the unconscious angel's wounds.

Daisuke had seen some things, but this was up there with the worst.

"I thought these lunatics worshipped an archangel?" Jinx said. "How could he allow them to do this to one of his own?"

"You'd have to take that up with the Binder," Daisuke said. "Let's get him down from there."

He climbed up on the altar and could just reach the

highest nail. As soon as he touched it he hissed and yanked his hand back. The black iron had burned his skin through his glove.

"Hell forged," Ruq said. "That's what's keeping the angel so weak. Can't imagine where archangel worshippers got such things."

"I'd say these aren't your average archangel worshippers," Carter said.

"Let's hope not," Daisuke said. "Anyone got a giant pair of pliers?"

It was a rhetorical question as of course no one did. With no better options, Daisuke took off his shirt, wrapped it five times around his right hand and tried again. It still stung, but not so much that he couldn't stand it.

Bracing one foot against the wall, he heaved for all he was worth. The nail came free and Daisuke somehow kept his balance. He tossed the nail aside and moved on to the next.

Once both wings were free and hanging limp from the angel's shoulders Daisuke said, "I'll need someone to support him."

Helena conjured bands of light around the angel's chest and legs.

With that taken care of, Daisuke got back to work. He was forced to wiggle the nail in the angel's right hand back and forth, drawing a groan as he made the wound bigger.

"Sorry about that."

With a final grunt of effort it came free. Thankfully the other nails weren't driven in as deeply and soon they had the unlucky angel safely on the floor.

Daisuke wiped sweat from his brow as Carter got busy healing the angel. That had taken more effort than flying here. He also needed a new shirt.

As he dug the metal card that allowed him to access his extra-dimensional storage out of his pocket Ruq said, "Handling the black iron is what wearied you. Hell-forged metal takes a toll on mortals just by being close to them."

"Great." Daisuke opened his trunk and pulled on a new shirt. "Jinx, could you do me a favor?"

"Of course."

He handed her his ruined shirt. "Wrap the black iron nails in that and I'll seal them in my trunk where they can't do any harm."

While she went to get the nails Daisuke stood and flexed his burned hand. Worked okay even if it still hurt a little.

"You'll need magical healing to repair the damage," Ruq said. "Wounds caused by hell-forged black iron won't heal on their own."

"That stuff is seriously bad news. Where would you even go to get it?"

"Hell?" Ruq suggested.

"These dazzling insights are exactly why I keep you around. Let me rephrase: where on Earth could they have gotten them?"

"No clue, Master."

"Right, well I suppose you *were* locked in a cage for heaven knows how long. Whatever, it's a problem for another day."

Jinx returned with the nails neatly wrapped in his old shirt and sealed with a band of shadow magic. He raised an eyebrow when he noticed that last bit.

She smiled. "I didn't want the bundle to come apart. That spell will hold for a week or so and since it's shadow magic, the black iron will make it stronger."

Daisuke took the bundle and tucked it deep in the trunk.

"That's perfect. If I'd thought of it, I'd have given you one of the nails to enhance your magic. Since you look so human, I keep forgetting you have demon blood."

She held up one of the nails. "That thought crossed my mind as well so I helped myself to one. You sure you don't mind if I keep it?"

"I trust you. Plus, when we catch up to the other Binder worshippers, we'll need every advantage we can get."

A groan from behind the altar prompted Daisuke to hurry over with Jinx on his heels. She'd tucked the nail away in her belt pouch.

The angel was working his way up the wall into a sitting position with Carter and Helena on either side of him. When he was comfortable, he looked at each of them in turn. When his gaze reached Jinx it lingered though Daisuke felt certain it was for different reasons than his usually did.

"You freed me?" the angel asked.

Carter nodded. "Are you feeling better?"

"Much, though I'm still weak. Those monsters left me nailed up there for weeks. The effects of the black iron won't wear off quickly. How did you find me?"

Carter explained what had happened so far. "I'm going to assume you're Xerxes. The boss was worried about you."

"Angelique is as close to a sister as I ever hope to have. You need to hurry and warn her. Since she didn't come to them, the remaining priests have gone to hunt her."

Daisuke was getting a queasy feeling. "Why, exactly, are members of the League of Mortals hunting the boss?" He had a pretty good idea, but wanted Xerxes to say it directly.

"Because Angelique is an angel."

CHAPTER SEVENTEEN

Daisuke ran a hand through his hair. Xerxes was still resting on the floor near the altar where they'd left him. Everyone else had gathered out of earshot to discuss the matters at hand, the main one being the boss's identity as an angel. To say that was a shock would be a vast understatement.

"Okay," he said. "Everyone that knew the boss was an angel raise your hand?"

When no one did he let out a sigh. "Great, at least I wasn't left out. Now I'm thinking I need to get back to Zurich and warn her ASAP."

"We should all go," Carter said. "Unfortunately, I can't teleport or shadow walk."

"Daisuke can take us," Helena said.

"No, I can't. I can take one of you and Jinx in my shadow, but that's it."

"That's fine," Jinx said. "I can take Carter and you take Helena. I'll follow you through the shadow paths."

Daisuke had never heard it called the shadow paths

before, but it was as good a name as any. Maybe as a half shadow demon she saw more than he did. She almost had to since he saw nothing at all.

"Sounds like a plan. Is he going to be okay?" Daisuke nodded toward the still-struggling angel.

"I'll be fine," Xerxes said. "My strength is slowly returning. I'll join you as soon as I'm recovered enough."

That answered that question and so much for moving out of earshot. Angels must have particularly good ears.

Daisuke spotted a large-enough shadow near the entrance and scooped Helena up in his arms.

"Hey! Can't I just hold your hand or something?"

"You can if you only want your arm to come with me. We need to be close enough for the spell to acknowledge us as one target. Relax, I won't drop you in the middle of the shadow realm."

"Shadow paths," Jinx said. She had Carter over her shoulder like a sack of potatoes and showed no difficulty holding him. He really needed to stop thinking of her like a normal woman.

"Right, shadow paths. Everyone ready?"

When they all indicated they were, he stepped into the shadow. A second later he emerged from the shadow of a dumpster outside Arcane Books and Trinkets. Daisuke set Helena down just as Jinx appeared beside him.

"Why didn't you appear in the safe room?" Helena asked.

"Jinx doesn't know how to bypass the wards. She would've been stuck in the shadow real... er, on the shadow paths."

Carter got busy unlocking the employees' entrance. While he did, Daisuke looked up and down the alley. There were a few people walking along the street, but none of them seemed to have noticed the group's arrival. That suited him fine. Even if it was a magic store, people just appearing out of nowhere was still rare enough to draw unwanted attention.

Get up on the roof and keep a lookout.

Before we return to that miserable desert, I want cookies.

Me too.

And cake and doughnuts.

Don't push it. Get up there.

He sensed Ruq fly up to the roof and look around. Joining his vision with his familiar's, Daisuke saw nothing that concerned him. The local cafes and businesses were busy, but not crazy at this time of the morning. There was nothing visible either in the real world or the ether that screamed "insane murder priest." Of course, if they'd been at this for any length of time, they were probably good at blending in. To make matters worse, he had no idea what they looked like.

Not exactly ideal.

He flinched when Helena touched his shoulder. "You were a million miles away."

"Actually, I was up on the roof. Ruq's on lookout duty. No sign of trouble yet."

Helena climbed the stairs up to the open door and he followed. "They wouldn't be crazy enough to attack the store in the middle of Zurich, would they?"

"Smashing up the house of innocent bystanders didn't do much to dissuade Deal. Let's just say I'm not optimistic."

"We need to get the boss and get out of the city." Helena closed and sealed the door behind him. "I can't even imagine the civilian casualties if we fight here."

Daisuke could but didn't particularly want to. The group

made the short walk to the boss's closed office door and Carter knocked.

"Come in," the boss said.

A haze of smoke filled the room. She'd been hitting the coffin nails hard this morning. Knowing her true nature, Daisuke worried far less about lung damage.

The boss was looking particularly charming today with her ash-gray hair pulled back in a neat ponytail. She even smiled, though as soon as her gaze settled on Jinx, it vanished.

"I see a new face, a pretty one too. Aren't you going to introduce me?"

"Sorry," Daisuke said. "Angelique, this is Jinx; Jinx, our boss, Angelique."

All the boss's good cheer was gone now. "I take it you met Xerxes."

"Yeah, we found him nailed to the wall of a Binder temple with hell-forged black iron nails. The people that did it are in Zurich looking for you since you didn't come to rescue your old pal the angel after they kidnapped him."

"I'm sensing annoyance, Daisuke," the boss—no, Angelique—said.

"Must be those keen heavenly senses. Did the whole angel thing slip your mind?"

"It's a long story and if the priests are here, I have no time to tell it now. I'll lead them out of the city and deal with them."

"Not alone you won't," Daisuke said. "Damned if I'm going to let you get yourself killed before you give me a proper explanation. An explanation over hot chocolate and the most expensive desserts in the city, your treat."

"I don't know about the rest, but we certainly aren't going to let you fight these lunatics on your own, boss," Carter said.

Angelique's hard expression softened. "I never doubted you, any of you, for a moment."

Three men are approaching the front door, Master.

"Shit."

"Daisuke?" Helena asked.

"We've got incoming. Where do you want to have this fight? I'll make the challenge while you all bounce."

"Do you remember the clearing I took you to when we first met?" Angelique asked.

"The one north of the city?"

"Yes. It's far enough away to be safe."

"Alright, get out of here."

"I'm staying with you." Before he could argue Jinx vanished into his shadow.

Angelique raised an eyebrow, but Daisuke shook his head. Another conversation for later.

He left the office and made his way to the front of the store. He reached the checkout counter just as the door opened and three men, the priests he assumed, entered. They were all dressed in dark suits and looked more like business-men, or maybe members of an organized crime syndicate, than priests. The clerk on duty looked at him and Daisuke nodded toward the back. "Get in the safe room and lock the door. Don't open it until I tell you."

The wide-eyed girl ran as if her life depended on it. She wasn't a wizard working a part-time job but an actual clerk that manned the store full time. She and another girl basi-cally ran the business part of their cover. Angelique had trained them both well and they knew when one of the special employees told them to hide, they'd better do it quickly.

The others have exited out the back.

Good. Hold your position. I don't want anyone sneaking up on me.

When the priests reached him, Daisuke said, "Welcome. I assume Father Deal recommended our store to you. Is there anything I can help you find?"

The three men shared looks. Whatever they'd been expecting, it wasn't this.

"You know Father Deal?" the center man asked. His eyes were so blue they reminded Daisuke of sapphire chips.

"We met, briefly. Unfortunately, he cut his own throat before we had a chance to talk in depth. If you three would do something similar, it would save me and my friends a lot of trouble."

The right-hand priest slammed his fist on the counter hard enough to make it rattle. "Where is the abomination? We know she lives here. Bring her out and you may live. Our quarrel is with the supernatural monstrosities polluting our world, not deluded humans."

"I appreciate your consideration, however the boss has stepped out for the day. If you'd still like to see her, I can offer directions. Somewhere outside the city. Don't you think that would be better for our discussion?"

"You seem awfully calm given your situation," the center priest said. "Perhaps if we take you hostage, she'll come to us."

Daisuke poured ether into the counter, or more specifically a series of invisible runes engraved into the surface. The shop's many defensive and offensive wards crackled to life. The three priests looked in every direction, seeming uncertain where the threat was coming from.

"While we prefer to keep things peaceful, this shop is not without protections. You will not find it easy to kidnap me."

"Enough," the left-hand priest finally said. "You swear to lead us to the angel?"

Daisuke made a little X over his heart. "Will you swear in the Binder's name to leave the shop peacefully and go directly to the battleground?"

The left-hand priest nodded. "In the Binder's name I swear."

Daisuke shifted his gaze to the other two and raised an eyebrow. After a bit of grumbling, they swore as well.

"Great. There's a clearing north of the city. It's not an official park, but you can't miss it, the field must be a mile across. We'll be waiting for you there."

"One more question if I may," the left-hand priest said. He looked like the oldest, at least if the streaks of gray in his short brown hair were any indication.

Daisuke nodded for him to continue.

"Why would you risk your life for this creature? It's not even human."

"Angelique is more human than plenty of actual humans I've met over the years. Her origin, or bloodline, or whatever, doesn't interest me in the least, only her actions matter. She's done more good for the world than you clowns can imagine. Is there anything else?"

"No," the leader said. "Thank you for answering my question. I can't understand your thinking and you clearly can't understand mine. Trial by combat will decide which of us is right, as in ancient times."

"Sure. It's about a two-hour hike to the clearing. See you there."

Without another word the priests walked back out just as calm as you please. When the door closed behind them Jinx appeared.

"You handled that with remarkable calm."

He grinned and got busy powering down the wards. "I was calmer on the outside than I was on the inside. It helped knowing you were here to back me up. The wards are every bit as powerful as I said, but we don't want to use them given how much damage the shop would take. A big fight might also convince the city council to kick us out, which would be a huge inconvenience. The oldest man seemed reasonable for a lunatic. Can't say I was expecting that."

"The most dangerous crazy people are the ones that don't realize they're crazy. So my father used to say."

The last ward deactivated and he turned toward the back. He needed to let the clerk know it was safe.

"Your father sounds very wise."

"I don't know about that. He thought all humans were crazy. He was as bad as those priests in his way."

"On the contrary, I agree with his assessment. Most humans are crazy in some way, myself included. At least he didn't run around killing them. He didn't, right?"

"No, Father only killed humans that bothered us."

"Perfectly reasonable policy." Daisuke knocked on the safe-room door. "You're good to get back to work."

The clerk opened the door and a nervous face peeked out. "Thank you, sir."

She slipped out and hurried up to her post. Daisuke didn't know her name and she didn't know his. That made things safer for everyone.

"Let's collect Ruq and get moving. I want to set up a few surprises before they reach the clearing."

F ather Elias and his brothers had put three blocks between themselves and the shop before he said, "That was disappointing. Why is it so many people refuse to see the truth about these creatures? Just because they look human doesn't mean they belong in this world."

"Most people prefer to stick their heads in the sand rather than face the truth," Father Michael said. "It has always been so and will always be so. That's why it's up to those of us that can see the truth to act. However many generations it takes, we will purify this world."

Elias appreciated Michael's enthusiasm even if his anger sometimes got the better of him. It seemed the best warriors seldom made the best diplomats.

"Do you think that kid was telling the truth about Deal?" Father Chase asked.

"I sensed no lie when he spoke," Elias said. "And any of us would do the same rather than risk important information being extracted during questioning. I fear we must accept the truth that our brother is dead. Once the angel is dealt with, we'll need to begin training a replacement."

"Do we have any candidates?" Michael asked. "That crazy nun in Warina doesn't strike me as a particularly good fit."

"No," Elias agreed. "Sister Eve's enthusiasm is laudable, but she's far too unstable. We're going to have to make a serious search at the different parishes to find someone."

"Forget that for now," Chase said. "You know we're walking into a trap, right?"

"Likely," Elias agreed. "But it doesn't matter. With our master's power to call upon, there's no chance that the three of us can lose. We will kill the angel and any who dare stand in our way."

"I'll wager Deal thought something similar," Michael said.

"Has your faith been shaken, Brother?" Elias asked.

"My faith is as strong as ever, I just think walking directly into a trap might not be the wisest decision."

"We swore on the master's name," Chase said. "If we fail to appear, it will be an insult to the Binder. No matter what, that can't be allowed."

"True," Elias said. "And more importantly, we know where the angel is now. If we fail to take this opportunity, it might flee, forcing us to hunt it down a second time—a far more difficult task now that it knows we exist. We are committed now, brothers. Let there be no more doubts and questions. The angel will die in the Binder's name."

The others made the chain symbol over their hearts and said in unison, "In the Binder's name."

CHAPTER EIGHTEEN

Daisuke emerged from the shadow of a tree beside a field he hadn't seen in a long time. The grass was knee high already and a healthy green. He took a breath of fresh air and sighed. Pity the stink of blood would soon be fouling the air.

Jinx appeared beside him and smiled. "What a beautiful spot."

"It really is. We should have a picnic here sometime. Not many city folk come this far out."

Angelique and the others had gathered in the center of the field. As the pair walked over to join them, Daisuke mused on the best traps to lay. He had to be careful since any spells he cast ahead of time would weaken him for the final battle.

"Can your shadows hide in the solid ground?"

"Certainly. They have no physical form. Why?"

"I thought you might hide a few here and there and have them grab an enemy ankle as he passed. It might not do much beyond slow them down, but any little advantage would be valuable."

"How many should I summon?"

"I'll leave that to your judgement."

She smiled at him in a sweet, almost bashful way.

"What?"

"Nothing, I just like how you trust me. It's not a reaction I'm used to getting and I like it."

"You've proven yourself worthy of trust. Rest assured it's not something I hand out lightly." When they reached the others he said, "They're coming. Sworn in the Binder's name."

"Good," Angelique said. "We can end it here. One less group of lunatics running around can only be a good thing. That said, from everything you've told me they won't go down easy. While the others prepare, Daisuke, you'll come with me to the vault."

"Do we really have time for a side trip?" he asked.

"It won't take long. I told you once that you'd have to visit the vault eventually. Now's the time." She held out her hand.

Daisuke shrugged and grasped it.

Black feathered wings appeared on her back.

She pulled him close and wrapped them both up in them.

A moment of dizziness quickly passed and he found himself standing in a narrow pass. At the end of it was a massive door built into a mountain. On either side were machine gun turrets equipped with actuators and laser sights. Weird that there would be such mundane defenses instead of magic.

"How come your wings aren't white?" he asked.

"I'm a fallen angel, cast out of Heaven for my crimes. Come on, I'll introduce you to the guardian computer."

Angelique walked right toward the door. "Keep up, Daisuke, or the computer might not recognize you as my guest."

He hurried to walk beside her. As soon as he took a step Ruq shimmered into view as he landed with a little thud in the dirt. He had reverted to his humanoid imp form.

"You okay?" Daisuke asked.

"I can't use my magic here."

Angelique paused and turned back. "No one can. This is a magic dead zone. Some force prevents the ether from entering this valley. Magical creatures will also lose their immunity to mundane weapons. It's the perfect place to house dangerous magical weapons."

"That explains the machine guns." He picked Ruq up and put him on his shoulder. He seemed heavier than usual, probably because he wasn't using his magic to reduce his weight. "What are we after, boss?"

"A weapon, one only you can control."

Daisuke didn't like where this was going. "You don't mean…"

"Yes, Vorgon. White wolves are dangerous enemies and those three priests can likely summon at least a dozen between them. I don't see how we can emerge unscathed from such a battle given our forces. The elder demon will make short work of them. And if he's killed in the process, well, that's hardly a great loss for the world."

"Can't argue with that. Still, are you sure this is a good idea?"

"I'm not going to lose any of you if I can avoid it. This is the less risky option."

They stopped outside the door and a green light scanned Angelique from head to toe. "Registered user identified. You may enter," a digital voice said.

"Computer, prepare to register a second authorized user."

"Acknowledge. New user registration program booting up." A beep sounded. "Registrant, approach."

Daisuke swallowed hard and moved to stand beside Angelique. The green light ran all over his body until another beep sounded.

"Registration complete. Input user name."

"Daisuke Kugo," Angelique said.

"Registration complete. Welcome, users." The door clunked then opened on its own.

Light flickered to life and they walked down a short hallway to a massive domed chamber lined with thousands of niches. Several hundred of them were already filled with a variety of weapons, scrolls, tomes, and other magical odds and ends. Vorgon's prison sat in one section all by its lonesome.

Angelique walked over and grabbed it. "Let's get back."

"What did you do to get kicked out of Heaven?"

"We don't have time."

"Take the time. If I might end up dead, I'd like to know the truth."

She kept walking toward the exit, but slowly. "I loved a mortal man. He was murdered. I found the one that did it and murdered her. My wings turned black and I was banished."

"Seriously? Seems excessive for killing one person. I've killed way more people than that, so I'm probably in real trouble."

She stopped and turned back to look him right in the eye. "It wasn't that I killed one person. It's that I murdered her for my own selfish reasons. Bringing a villain to justice gets you a heavenly reward. Avenging your lover in a fit of rage is the act of a demon, not an angel."

"Sounds like bullshit to me. Considering what the Binder lets his followers get away with, I don't have much respect for whoever's running things up there."

Her stern expression finally softened. "Thanks, Daisuke."

They emerged from the vault and she said, "All defenses engage."

The computer beeped and the door swung shut. As soon as they reached the edge of the magic dead zone, she took Daisuke's hand again and wrapped her wings around him.

Helena, Carter, and Jinx stood around staring at each other. With Daisuke and the boss gone to get who knew what from the vault, Helena wasn't sure what that should be doing. Finally she turned to Carter, more to fill the uncomfortable silence than anything.

"Is there anything we should be doing to get ready?"

Carter shook his head. "Without knowing exactly where the enemy is coming from, we can't waste magic on traps."

"I summoned a few shadows and had them hide in the ground," Jinx said. "Though given how poorly they fared in the last fight, it's probably a waste of time."

"You're the expert on all things heavenly," Helena said. "How do we stop these things?"

"I'm not sure there's much we can do," Carter said. "White wolves are powerful heavenly spirits, beast angels I suppose you could call them. Only the golden lions that guard Heaven's gate are more powerful. They'll absorb my light magic without taking damage. A powerful barrier might slow them, but it would have to be your strongest and even then I wouldn't expect more than a slight delay. Their divine aura will burn through Jinx's shadow magic, though given enough time it will hurt them."

"My sisters and I killed a few of them when we combined our power, but it exhausted us in a hurry."

"So basically all we can do is rely on Daisuke and whatever weapon he and the boss bring back?" Helena asked. "I don't particularly like the sound of that."

Carter shrugged. "Whether you like it or not changes nothing. Some enemies are just a bad matchup for you. I'll be focusing on healing, just in case anyone gets hurt. The best advice I can give you is to be ready and do what you can without getting in the way."

Helena ground her teeth but knew Carter was right. That didn't mean she had to like it.

An instant after the boss wrapped her wings around Daisuke, they were back in the clearing. Everything looked exactly as they'd left it.

"What was that all about?" Helena asked. Her eyes widened when she saw what the boss was holding. "You can't be serious."

"As a brain tumor." Daisuke summoned his storage trunk and brought out the Staff of Law. Vorgon's seal looked unchanged from when he put it in place. "I'll take the prison."

Angelique handed it to him. "Don't summon Vorgon until they're close. The longer he's free, the more it will take out of you."

"I'm in no rush, boss."

"Still planning to stick with me despite my forgetting to mention that I wasn't human?"

"Considering some of the humans I've met, I can't hold that against you. We've done some good; maybe if we collect all seventy-two demons, we can get those wings bleached and send you home."

She chuckled. "All things considered, I'm in less of a rush to return than I used to be. I still can't imagine what the other archangels are thinking, letting the Binder and his followers run wild like this."

Angelique cocked her head and Daisuke sensed it a moment later. They were coming, far sooner than he expected.

"Now, Daisuke. Everyone else stay beside me."

The group shifted so Daisuke stood a little bit in front of everyone else. He charged the staff with ether, focusing it on Vorgon's seal.

Power arced from the staff to the prison. The demon's black presence oozed through Daisuke's mind. He was eager. Half-heard whispers demanded he let him loose. Even softer whispers promised to make him a god on earth if he'd only set him free.

Shut up!

Vorgon's presence flinched away from his command.

Good, the demon understood who was in charge.

White wolves emerged from the edge of the woods. Three of them were as big as horses and the priests rode on their backs like that girl from the ancient anime.

"Time to go to work." Daisuke tapped the prison. "Vorgon! In the name of Solomon you are summoned. By my blood and the power of the staff you are bound. Slay my enemies! Let none of them survive!"

The priests and their beasts charged.

A great black cloud of corruption billowed out of the prison.

Thunder cracked and day became night.

A giant figure formed in front of Daisuke. Black scales rippled over bulging muscles.

With a snap of his bat wings Vorgon raced toward the approaching white wolves.

One of the smaller ones leapt at him.

An almost causal backhand sliced the beast in half, destroying it.

Daisuke focused all his will on the link between himself and Vorgon. The demon needed little coaxing to kill the servants of Heaven. He rent their flesh with unholy glee, all of which washed over Daisuke through their connection.

He was going to need to wash his brain when this job was done.

Two of the priests on their giant mounts led the surviving white wolves in a direct attack on Vorgon. When they were fully engaged, the third rode alone toward Daisuke. And there wasn't a thing he could do about it.

Helena wasn't exactly sure what to think when she finally understood what Daisuke and the boss were planning. Intentionally opening the demon prison and letting Vorgon out went against everything they'd been told. But seeing the monster in action, she was forced to admit that he made a potent ally. And while she certainly didn't trust Vorgon, she did trust Daisuke.

She also loved him. Seeing him with Jinx had finally made

her feelings painfully clear to her. She flicked a glance at her rival and found the half demon chewing on her lip as she watched Daisuke. Though Jinx hadn't known him as long, Helena had no doubt that Jinx's feelings ran every bit as deep as her own. How they were going to resolve that was a matter for later.

One of the priests guided his wolf around the knot of battle and urged it directly at them. He was totally focused on Daisuke. Clearly he understood who was controlling the demon.

Shadowy hands sprang out of the ground and grasped at the huge wolf's legs.

It smashed right through them, taking no damage, and not even slowing.

Keeping Carter's warning in mind, Helena used all her might to conjure a barrier of pure golden ether a hundred yards out.

The wolf smashed through that with the same ease it had the shadow hands.

Carter's light magic blasts didn't so much as singe its fur.

This was pathetic. Just one priest was going to kill them all before Vorgon went on a rampage.

Only fifty yards separated them from the charging wolf.

Helena readied another barrier. Damned if she was going down without giving all she had.

Something rustled behind her and the boss brushed past her to stand directly in the wolf's path. Her raven wings snapped open and ether gathered around them.

The power built until the white wolf was only three strides away.

At last her wings snapped forward.

Black feathers rode hurricane-force winds right at the approaching beast.

They hit like daggers, carving into both the wolf and its rider, slicing them open and finally sending the wolf crashing to the ground. Before they could move Vorgon stomped on the fallen pair, reducing them to bloody mush.

"Back to your prison, Vorgon!" Daisuke's voice boomed like thunder over the battlefield.

Vorgon roared and twisted as chains of ether wrapped around his body and dragged him foot by foot back to the bronze cylinder.

"I will not go back!" Vorgon roared.

"You will! By my will and the power of the seal, be bound. By the blood of Solomon and the might of the Staff of Law, Vorgon, be bound in bronze."

An inarticulate howl of pure rage exploded out of the demon. Helena nearly collapsed, her body trembling at the sheer magnitude of the corruption being released.

Through the storm Daisuke stood straight and unbending, waves of evil crashing against him like the ocean against a cliff. He took everything Vorgon could throw at him until the last of the demon had vanished into the cylinder.

With a final tap of the staff, the darkness fully vanished. The sky cleared and everyone breathed a sigh of relief.

"I don't know how Solomon did it," Daisuke said a moment before he collapsed.

The boss caught him and laid him gently in the grass. A faint smile curved her lips as she brushed a finger across his cheek.

Did Helena have another rival to worry about?

She immediately dismissed the idea as irrelevant and hurried over. "Is he okay?"

"Yes, just tired. Channeling that much ether combined with withstanding Vorgon's corruption is a lot to ask of anyone. Daisuke handled it better than wizards twice his age with ten times the experience. That said, I won't be asking him to free a demon anytime soon. Can the three of you get him home? I need to return Vorgon's prison to the vault."

"I've got a key to his apartment, so no problem," Helena said.

"I'll join you later," Carter said. "I want to check the bodies and see if there are any clues about the League of Mortals."

"I thought this was all of them," Jinx said.

"That's our assumption," Carter said. "But we don't actually know. I also need to call my brother. I asked him to check in on Bido while we were gone."

With everything that had happened, Helena had forgotten all about the Aborigine Daisuke rescued. They still needed to go back and find the leaking prison, but that would keep until Daisuke recovered. In fact, it had to wait. He was the only one that could wield the staff.

Speaking of which. "Boss, what do you want me to do with the Staff of Law?"

"Take it with you, but don't try and use it. The staff wouldn't be pleased if you did."

Helena nodded and conjured a golden disk under Daisuke, lifting him gently off the ground. Looked like they were going to have to walk back to the parking lot then call a cab. Helena had never been good at flying magic, but after this mission, she was determined to improve.

She set out for the city with Daisuke floating between her and Jinx. Helena didn't bother to tell Jinx she didn't need to tag along. She imagined it wouldn't do any good if she did.

The three of them reached a wide parking lot and found it just as empty as when they arrived. That suited Helena perfectly as having to explain what happened to Daisuke was a conversation she'd prefer to avoid.

A quick call secured a cab. Now it was just a matter of waiting.

"Will he be okay?" Jinx touched Daisuke's cheek and sighed.

"He will be fine." Ruq's voice came from directly above Daisuke's chest. "My master is far too sturdy to let something like this lay him low for long. When he wakes up, he'll want hot chocolate, cookies, cake, and doughnuts."

"Isn't that what you wanted?" Helena asked.

"Yes, but I'm willing to share with him."

Jinx reached out and patted the air. "You're an excellent familiar."

"Finally, someone that appreciates my many qualities. I'll be recommending he focus his attention on you, rather than the demon hater."

"Hey! Hating demons is normal, especially ones that look like rats and have bad table manners." She turned to Jinx. "No offense."

Jinx smiled and stopped petting Ruq. "None taken. After all, I'm only half demon and I have excellent table manners. What happens next?"

"Once Daisuke wakes up, we need to return to Australia and find the demon prison."

"I was thinking more long-term, you know, with the three of us." Jinx's brow furrowed. "And did you see the way that angel looked at him?"

"Right? I think the boss might have a thing for Daisuke."

"I can understand why. He's been very kind to me. I hope I can eventually pay him back for all he's done."

"My master will be pleased to hear that. I know several things you could do that would make him very happy."

"You stay out of this," Helena said. "It's a matter between women."

As the cab pulled into the parking lot Helena said, "We'll discuss this more once we're somewhere private."

"Agreed."

CHAPTER NINETEEN

Daisuke groaned and sat up in bed. His bed. That was a good sign. The fact that he couldn't remember how he got here was less encouraging. It was getting to be a habit. Daylight streamed in under his curtains. How long had he been out?

"Only six hours, Master. Your tolerance for corruption is improving."

"Is that good or bad?"

"Given what you do for a living, I'd say good." Ruq climbed up on the bed in rat form. "Mention has been made of sweets when you wake up. If you could hurry and get dressed, I'd like to eat them."

Daisuke threw the covers off and conjured a light. The Staff of Law leaned in one corner and his clothes had been neatly folded across the back of a chair. Helena must've undressed him, but it was rare to see her leaving things so neat.

"Jinx folded your clothes. However, they reek of demon

essence, so I'd recommend the laundry basket or an incinerator.

"Helena let Jinx come back with her? That's a surprise."

"It's less that she was allowed and more that Jinx insisted on coming along. She was very nice to me, unlike the demon hater. I suggest you swap females."

Relationship advice from a demon, exactly what he needed right now. He rolled out of bed, collected clothes from the closet, and dressed. His wallet and the token that summoned his trunk were still in his pants pockets, so he swapped them over. He needed to put the staff away as well.

Preparations complete, he stepped out into the living room where he found Jinx and Helena sitting in silence on opposite sides of the living room.

"Should I go back to bed?"

"No, you should call the bakery and get us goodies." Ruq had flown up onto the kitchen counter.

He tossed his phone to Ruq then turned to look from Jinx to Helena. "Thanks for bringing me back. As soon as I eat, we can return to work."

"First things first," Helena said. "What are your intentions going forward?"

Daisuke cocked his head. "My intentions? Did we just jump back in time a thousand years? The only intentions I have are to finish finding the demon prisons. We've still got seventy-one to go. Assuming I can do that and survive, then I'll think about my future. Unless you two have suggestions."

"I think Helena wants to know which of us is going to be your girlfriend," Jinx said.

Daisuke stared at the two of them. This couldn't be happening. They were members of a secret society dedicated to finding and sealing away dangerous magical artifacts. This wasn't high school. In fact, Daisuke hadn't had a conversation this stupid even when he was in high school. Unfortunately for him, it seemed they were both serious.

"Look, I like you both and have no intention of choosing between you unless you force me to. And if you're planning to force me to, then I'll choose neither of you. I can't deal with this emotional bullshit and do my job. If you want to have fun between missions, I'm cool with that. If you're looking to play house and pick out plates and throw pillows, forget it."

Both women were staring at him with their mouths partway open. Maybe that had been a little bit brusque. But heaven's mercy, he did not want to deal with this right now.

"The goodies will be here in fifteen minutes," Ruq announced.

"Thank the universe. I need sugar in the worst way."

He was rummaging through the cupboards when his phone rang.

"It's the angel," Ruq said.

Daisuke took the phone. "Yeah, boss."

"Happy to hear you're back among the living. Carter just got off the phone with his brother. We've got serious problems."

"Of course we do. Are these 'get to the office immediately' problems or 'stuff yourself with carbs and then come to the office' problems?"

She chuckled. "After all the magic you used, you'll need the calories. Eat fast then get over here. Bring Helena with you. Carter and I will be waiting."

"Gotcha, boss. Half an hour, tops."

"What's up?" Helena asked. For the moment at least it sounded like she was over the romance drama.

"Trouble down under. Five will get you ten it's werewolf related. This is what happens when there are too many loose ends."

Murder priests, demons, and werewolves. He'd happily deal with any or all of them if it avoided further conversations about relationships.

Five thousand calories' worth of sugar did wonders for Daisuke's energy level. As soon as they finished eating, he teleported everyone to the shop safe room. A short walk brought them to the boss's office.

Daisuke knocked and a moment later the boss said, "Come in."

She was seated behind her desk with Carter at her right shoulder. A map was spread out across the desk and the pair was giving it a serious look.

"So what's the big problem, boss?" Daisuke asked.

"Werewolves have invaded Warina," Carter said. "Anson brought Bido back with him when he went to check in. A few hours later forty-plus werewolves showed up. The people have locked themselves in their homes and for the moment the focus seems to be our place, where Bido is holed up. Guns can't kill them, but at least the bullets seem to hurt the brutes. It's a standoff for now, but there's no way that'll last."

"What do you want to bet that's every member of the fourth tribe?" Daisuke asked.

"I suspect you're right," Carter said. "But the source of the werewolves is less important than dealing with them."

"Has anyone seen any sign of the prison?" Daisuke asked.

"Anson didn't mention it or anything that sounded like it."

That was too much to hope for. "Sounds like we've got a town to rescue. Assuming Jinx is willing to help us out again, we can be there in a snap."

"I'd be happy to," Jinx said.

"Are you planning to carry me over your shoulder again?" Carter asked.

"Would you prefer a bridal carry?" Jinx asked.

Carter grimaced. "On second thought, over the shoulder is fine."

Daisuke grinned. "Call Anson, tell him we're coming, and that we'll appear in the living room from the shadow of the second-floor stairs. It would make me very happy if no one shot us when we arrived."

"I didn't even think about that. Good call." Carter whipped out his phone and dialed. "Anson promises not to shoot us."

Carter moved over to join them. "Everyone ready?"

When they all indicated they were the boss said, "Good luck."

CHAPTER TWENTY

Daisuke emerged from the shadow cast from the stairs to the second floor and stepped into the middle of the Monk family living room. Not exactly ideal, but it was the biggest shadow he could find in the room. Jinx joined him a moment later.

"That's a hell of an entrance," Anson said from the shattered remains of the front door.

"It got the job done," Daisuke said. "What's the situation?"

"We're in here, they're out there. Every once in a while one of the ugly buggers pops into view and I try and shoot it. When I succeed it yelps and ducks back out of sight. Far as I can tell, all I'm doing is bruising the bloody things."

"I can fix that." Carter went over and passed his index finger along the barrel of Anson's lever-action rifle, causing glowing runes to appear. "There, every bullet for the next hour will gain an enchantment. Should be enough to overcome their damage resistance."

"Now we're talkin'. Dad's watching the back door. Might want to do the same for him."

"I will." Carter strode off into the kitchen.

"Where's Bido?" Daisuke asked.

"Upstairs in the guest bedroom." Anson snapped up his rifle and fired off a shot. "Bugger! I missed him. As soon as he saw the werewolves he fainted dead away. Haven't heard a peep from him since."

"That might work to our advantage. Jinx, Helena, if you two don't mind helping out down here, I'm going to collect a blood sample."

"For the spell you told me about?" Jinx asked.

"Yes. I need to deal with the big boss. If he gets away, even if we kill all the werewolves, he'll just make more."

"We'll be fine," Helena said. "Get going."

Daisuke left the living room, found a flight of stairs, and climbed them. At the top he found a row of doors. Behind the first one was an empty bedroom. Behind the second he found Bido curled up on the bed in the fetal position, trembling and whimpering. That was much worse than unconscious. Why didn't he grab Justine to translate?

He shook his head. There wasn't time to screw around.

A paralysis spell rendered Bido immobile.

Daisuke went in and tapped Bido's shoulder. A tiny spark shot out and pricked the dark skin, letting a single drop of blood well up. He collected that in a bubble of ether before making another pass with his hand, closing up the tiny wound.

"I apologize for this, but it's necessary if we want to end the current situation. I'm sure you have no idea what I'm saying, but I wanted to say it anyway." He nodded to Bido and released his spell.

The man stared at him until Daisuke backed out and closed the door. He had serious doubts about Bido's future mental stability, but there was nothing he could do about that now. Or later for that matter. Daisuke's magic was geared toward direct confrontation. Dealing with the subtleties of the mind were beyond him.

Turning his focus on the blood, Daisuke charged it with ether then let a thread out. This spell was called Blood Hunter and it did exactly what it sounded like. The thread streaked away toward the north. That way, huh?

He stopped it before it went too far and returned to the living room. A rifle cracked from the kitchen. Given the infrequency of the shots, it was safe to assume no major attack had happened yet.

"The shaman is somewhere north of here. I'll deal with him and seal the prison. That will likely either cause the remaining werewolves to drop dead or go into a frenzy, so be on your guard."

Helena and Jinx both stared at him. The worry in their eyes was both obvious and heartwarming, but he couldn't let it keep him from doing what he had to.

"Wish me luck." Daisuke headed for the front door.

As soon as he was outside, he cast a flying spell and turned north. The Blood Hunter guided him outside the town. About a hundred yards from the last building, he spotted four huge werewolves surrounding a small, wizened Aborigine who crackled with corruption. He clutched the demon prison to his chest like it was the most precious thing in the world to him. And given how badly the corruption had twisted him, it might've been.

The werewolves growled and snarled, baring their fangs. At least they couldn't fly.

Daisuke pointed at the nearest one and the black disk

appeared under its feet. Black lightning shot up, blasting through its body and burning the life out of it.

One of the others leapt, but came up five yards short of reaching him.

The shaman brandished the prison at Daisuke like it was a holy talisman and Daisuke was a vampire to be driven away.

It was sad to see someone so far gone.

His pity nearly cost him.

A blast of corruption shot out of the prison.

Daisuke dropped straight down to avoid it, but still gagged as the darkness passed over his head.

The werewolves chose that moment to strike.

They leapt, snagging his legs and pulling him to the ground.

Daisuke winced as their claws scrabbled against his ethereal barrier. The beasts couldn't penetrate it, but their corruption still sickened him.

Gathering his power, Daisuke lashed out.

Black lightning exploded in every direction, lancing through the werewolves and burning their life away.

When he stood, only smoldering corpses remained.

Master!

Daisuke leapt forward and rolled, evading another blast of corruption by inches.

He came to his feet, spun, and hurled more lightning at the shaman.

A dark barrier absorbed the spell.

Daisuke didn't let up.

Blast after blast hammered into the barrier.

Cracks formed.

Finally, it shattered.

Before the shaman could recover, a black disk appeared under his feet. A massive lightning bolt roared out of it, reducing the man to ash.

Daisuke dropped to his knees and blew out a long breath. Okay, that ended up being harder than expected. While he rested, Daisuke pulled the metal card out of his pocket and summoned his trunk. He collected the staff and stood.

Time to finish this.

Standing over the prison, there was no doubt that it was still oozing corruption. He touched it with the staff and soon found the damaged area of the binding.

Unfortunately, when he tried to repair it, nothing happened.

"Damn it!" He must need the seal before he could fix the hole in the binding.

"What now, Master?" Ruq asked.

"Now we need to find the seal. With my luck it's probably halfway around the world. Do me a favor and fly back to Warina and see if the werewolves are still active. I'm not sure if the shaman was controlling them or the demon."

Ruq turned invisible and Daisuke sensed him moving away. He sat a comfortable distance away from the prison and took deep breaths. Thank heaven for that big breakfast. On the downside, he was already hungry again.

They're still fighting, Master. Though it looks like the Monk house is no longer their focus.

Figures, now that the shaman is dead, the demon probably doesn't care about Bido. I'm going to try and create a secondary barrier. Let me know what happens.

Daisuke channeled ether through the staff and created a bubble around the prison. He made it as thick as possible and soon the corruption started to build up. The pure ether dissolved and only by constantly repairing the barrier was he able to keep it intact.

No change in the werewolves' behavior. I looked closer and it seems the curse has been altered. They resemble thralls now more than cursed men.

That explains a lot. Thanks.

If the werewolves were actually thralls, then they'd just keep fighting until destroyed regardless of what happened with the prison. Given that, wasting his strength on a temporary barrier was pointless.

Best to go help with the fight then hunt down the seal he needed to properly repair the prison.

He reached for the prison then froze. Holding an artifact leaking corruption would only weaken him. But it wasn't like he could just leave it lying in the middle of nowhere either. Much as he didn't want to, Daisuke summoned his trunk again and used an ethereal hand to deposit the prison inside.

Hopefully the corruption didn't melt his clothes. He kept the staff in hand since it provided a little power boost even outside its purpose of controlling and imprisoning Solomon's demons.

That done, Daisuke took to the air and rocketed back toward Warina.

At the very edge of town, he spotted a werewolf loping down the street. A burst of black lightning took care of it.

Nodding to himself, Daisuke went hunting. If he'd been the sort to care about a fair fight, he might've felt bad for the werewolves. They couldn't touch him from the ground and without someone controlling them, they were too stupid to do anything but run around in a frenzy looking for someone to attack.

The only thing he regretted as he burned them down one after another was the loss of the innocent men they used to be.

The sun had set by the time he finished off the last werewolf and landed in the Monk family compound. Sweat covered him and his legs were wobbly, but otherwise Daisuke felt fine.

Helena and Jinx emerged from the house but stopped a few feet away. They looked at each other as if uncertain how to proceed.

"Is anyone going to give me a hug?"

Ruq landed on his shoulder and wrapped his rat arms around Daisuke's neck. "Feel better, Master?"

"No. You're not my type."

Before the ladies could get themselves sorted out, Justine, Carter, and the rest of the Monk family joined them in the yard.

"Did you get it?" Carter asked.

"Yeah, the shaman is dead as are all the werewolves he created. At least all the ones in Warina are. It seems unlikely he just let some wander on their own."

"So it's over?" Anson asked.

"More or less," Daisuke said.

Anson scowled. "What does that mean?"

"It means Warina is safe, but that we've still got work to do. By us I mean myself and my coworkers. First we need to collect the bodies of anyone killed by the werewolves and burn them. Anyone injured needs to have their wounds checked for corruption and if any is present, it needs to be purified. Once that's done, I need to cast a tracking spell so I can find this prison's seal and use it to repair the leak. Last but not least I'm going home to sleep until the boss has another job for me."

"I can handle the wounded," Carter said.

"I'll help." Justine sounded eager to do something.

"I'll burn the bodies," Helena offered.

Daisuke nodded. "I appreciate that. I'm done for at least a few hours. My hope is that Mrs. Monk will let me raid her fridge and point me to a bed."

Carter's mom smiled. "I'll whip you up something. Any requests?"

"As long as it has a lot of calories, I don't care. This is basically just me visiting a gas station so to speak."

"I'll keep you company," Jinx said.

Helena didn't object which came as a surprise. Probably figured Daisuke was too tired to do anything anyway. And she wasn't wrong.

The group broke up and Daisuke followed the Monk family back inside with Jinx beside him. He didn't know how far he'd have to go to find the seal, but that was a problem for tomorrow. Right now, all he wanted was a home-cooked meal and about ten hours' sleep.

CHAPTER TWENTY-ONE

Daisuke woke to bright sunshine pouring through the guest-bedroom window. After a delicious meal and a good night's sleep, he felt ready to take on the final stage of the mission. He doubted the search for the seal would be quick, but he couldn't stop until the prison had been repaired. Speaking of which, it was going to be a pain casting the seeking spell with so much corruption clouding the ether.

As soon as he finished getting dressed, he went down-stairs and found everyone else already up and waiting for him around the kitchen table. A quick glance at the stove clock confirmed that it was already after ten.

"Finally up," Helena said. "You're worse than a teenager on a school day."

"I seldom slept in as a teenager. It's only since I started hunting demons that I find I need to sleep in from time to time. How'd the locals make out?"

"Better than we feared," Carter said. "Eight fatalities and

twenty wounded. Given the number of werewolves it could've been much worse."

"If they had a brain between them, it would've been. Thank heaven for stupid thralls." Daisuke glanced at the fridge. "I'll fix myself a quick breakfast and we can get started on the final leg of the mission."

"There's leftover bacon and Mom made fresh biscuits this morning," Carter said.

That sounded perfect and Daisuke got busy making himself some sandwiches.

When he finished eating Helena asked, "Can I see the prison?"

"Not here. It's leaking too much corruption. No way am I taking it out of extra-dimensional storage until we're out of town."

"Good call," Carter said. "The rest of the family and Justine are busy helping out around town, so we can go as soon as you're ready."

Daisuke nodded. "I'm ready."

They drove away from the Monk Compound in a borrowed off-road delivery truck and kept going until they reached a safe location five miles beyond the edge of town in the bleakest, most empty stretch of nothing Daisuke had ever seen. They got out of the truck and he summoned his trunk. Carefully wrapping the prison in a bubble of ether, he pulled it out so the others could take a look.

Not that there was much to see. It wasn't like the bronze cylinder had any marks on it. It was the magic that was damaged. You couldn't even see the corruption with normal vision.

"Not much to look at, is it?" Carter asked.

"Is this the first prison you've seen?" Daisuke asked.

"The first one I've seen in person. I've seen pictures and illustrations, but they don't really do it justice. And you were right, it's really leaking. I'm glad it's only a greater demon and not an elder."

"'Only' he says," Helena muttered.

"I'm just saying it could be worse."

Daisuke glanced at Jinx who hadn't said a word. Her already pale skin was bloodless as she stared at the cylinder.

"You okay?"

She dragged her gaze away from the cylinder and looked at him. "Yeah, that thing just reminds me of my dad a little. His aura was similar, but not quite as dark."

"He was a demon, even if a risen one. I guess that's not too surprising. If we're all done looking at the prison, what say I cast the seeking spell?"

When no one objected, he shaped the ether, connecting it to the prison. As he'd feared, the constant corruption made the spell unstable. Fortunately, using the staff mitigated that to some extent, allowing him to maintain the spell with only modest extra effort. The spell Daisuke used was a variation of the hound spell Haakon had cast in Japan. His didn't have an animal shape, instead it looked like a simple black tentacle that pointed toward the item he sought while also providing a vague idea of the distance separating him from it.

To his considerable surprise, the seal felt close.

"It's within a couple hundred miles."

"You're certain?" Carter asked.

"As certain as I can be."

"Then let's go."

They got back in and Carter drove while Daisuke sat beside him with the prison. Helena and Jinx were stuck in the back. Flying would've been faster, but he couldn't maintain both spells, especially with the corruption interfering.

The landscape didn't get any more interesting as they traveled. Hours passed in silence. No one wanted to interrupt his concentration which Daisuke appreciated. They were approaching some low hills when he sensed the seal was just ahead.

"We're getting close. The base of those hills I think."

"There's nothing out here," Carter said. "How would the seal have even gotten to a place like this?"

"It probably landed here when the last wielder of the staff died."

Carter gave him a curious look.

"Did the boss not tell you? There's an emergency spell on the staff that causes all the seals imbedded in it to scatter should the current wielder die without designating an heir."

"Smart. If anything happens to you, it'll keep Solomon the Great from gaining a bunch of demon seals in one go." Carter immediately realized what he'd implied and hastened to add, "Not that I think anything will happen to you."

"Relax, I know what you meant."

A hundred yards from the base of the hill was a little mound of earth. According to his spell, that's where the seal rested.

"You can stop."

"Where is it?" Carter asked.

Daisuke nodded toward the mound. "I'd say it's buried about three feet down."

"That looks suspiciously like a grave."

"My thoughts exactly."

Carter stopped and everyone got out. They gathered around the mound and stared at it.

"Anyone bring a shovel?" Helena asked.

It was a lame joke, but everyone chuckled all the same.

With some of the tension cleared, Carter and Helena conjured ethereal scoops and started removing dirt. The magic cut through the ground with almost no resistance and in ten minutes they'd exposed a partially decomposed corpse. It was dressed in typical explorer garb of khaki shorts and a tan shirt. From the breadth of the shoulders, Daisuke guessed it had been a man.

He released his seeking spell, bent down, and removed the seal from the dead man's shirt pocket. A quick check confirmed that the rune on the seal matched the prison.

Finally.

Daisuke placed the seal on the staff and whispered the spell to connect them. A moment later a smooth spot formed on the twisted surface with the rune in the center. Next he set the prison down and touched it with the staff. This time, when he tried to fix the leak, the magic leapt to obey. In less than a minute the damage was fully repaired and no corruption was visible.

Now all they had to do was take it to the vault.

"He wasn't a local." Helena had the dead man's wallet in her hand. "According to his license he was from France. Mr. Julian Pilat, age twenty-nine."

"Take anything you can find," Carter said. "There's no way the boss won't want us to look into this guy."

Helena searched the body for valuables and aside from his wallet found only a plain silver ring and a Celtic cross necklace.

"We need to get back," Daisuke said. "Are you coming, Carter?"

"Not right now. I'll take a week to help my family get

sorted out and figure out a cover story for Justine to tell the university."

"If you need a flight back," Daisuke said. "The Puddle Duck should still be waiting in Tasmania."

"Good to know, thanks. See you later."

Carter headed for the truck alone.

Daisuke turned to Jinx. "What do you say, want to try living in Zurich?"

"Yes, please. Living alone, in that cavern, doesn't appeal to me. Though I hate to impose on you after all you've done for me already."

"Not a problem. Besides, I'd have missed you something awful if you didn't want to join us."

Helena grimaced but was too polite to outright say she didn't want Jinx around.

"Let's find a shadow and head home."

CHAPTER TWENTY-TWO

Angelique nodded as Daisuke finished his report. That was two demon prisons in the vault and seventy to go. It sounded less impressive when you thought about it that way, but the truth was, the team's success was outstanding, especially given everything they'd faced.

She leaned back in her chair and reached for a cigarette. Halfway to the pack she caught herself. Daisuke grinned at her. Despite his initial annoyance that she hadn't told him the truth about her nature, he hadn't been treating her any differently. Angelique appreciated that. Some mortals, when faced with an actual angel, got funny ideas that they needed to be worshipped.

There were things she needed, but that wasn't one of them.

"You know, boss," Daisuke said. "If I'd known you were immortal, I wouldn't have given you so much grief about your smoking and dietary habits. Just out of curiosity, do you actually get a nicotine buzz?"

"No, it's just a habit I picked up from… It's just a habit."

Daisuke nodded without further comment, bless him. "So what's the next move?"

"Your next move is resting and getting Jinx settled. You do still trust her, right?"

"As much as I trust anyone. If she meant us harm, she's had plenty of chances to do something about it. I've got an apartment lined up for her in my building. Do I need to help her find a job, or will you hire her?"

"If we can trust her, she's too powerful to waste waiting tables or answering phones. You two will partner up for a year and then we'll decide for sure."

"Works for me. What about Helena? She spilt already."

"I sent her to France to investigate the dead man you found. At a bare minimum his family needs to be told what happened to him. Maybe it'll lead to something more and maybe not. Time will tell."

"Good enough. If you need me, you know how to reach me." Daisuke threw a wave over his shoulder as he left her office.

She smiled at his back.

A moment later a voice said, "Not terribly respectful."

Angelique turned to look at Xerxes who had let the illusion spell hiding him lapse. He had transformed into his preferred human form, that of a tall, slim man in a gray suit. "Not in the traditional sense, but Daisuke is one of the finest humans I've ever known. I got very lucky when I convinced him to join the Circle. Not to mention, if it wasn't for him, you'd still be nailed to the temple wall."

Xerxes winced. "You have me there. I was most grateful for the rescue."

"I'll bet. So, what about the book? Did you actually find it?"

"No, though I did find a clue that looks promising." Xerxes blew out a sigh. "I swear sometimes it feels like I'll need the rest of eternity to find the miserable book."

"If it takes you that long, then it probably won't matter if you actually succeed."

"That thought crossed my mind as well. Nevertheless, I can't stop now, not when I've invested so much time."

Angelique nodded. Stubbornness wasn't only a human failing after all. "What of the Binder? Will he continue to oppose us?"

"Who can say? You're a fallen angel; no doubt he considers you a mistake that needs cleaning up. As for me, I disobeyed a direct order and refused to return to Heaven. The fact that my wings are still white says that Heaven itself still favors me even if one of the archangels doesn't."

"The Binder always did think too highly of himself. You know he was cast out and only the efforts of a group of humans allowed him to be purified and return to Heaven."

"I do know. And if he can be redeemed, then so can you. You're doing good work, Angelique. I'm very proud."

Her lips twisted in a bitter smile. "I'm glad someone is. Do keep in touch."

Xerxes smiled back. His was bright, warm, and pure, as a proper angel's smile should be. "I will do my best, but you know how I get when I'm researching."

"Indeed I do. Goodbye, my dear friend."

"Goodbye, Angelique. The blessings of heaven be upon you." Xerxes vanished in a burst of white light.

"The blessings of heaven," she muttered. Worthless as they were, she wouldn't turn them down.

AUTHOR NOTE

Hello everyone,

Thanks very much for checking out A Friend in Need. I hope you enjoyed Daisuke's latest adventure as well as meeting Jinx. She'll be playing a large part in the series going forward.

And speaking of that, the adventure continue in The Demon Masks, coming soon. If you like to be notified about all my new releases as well as any deals or discounts be sure to sign up for my newsletter here. https://www.jamesewisher.com

Thanks for reading,

James

ALSO BY JAMES E WISHER

The 72 Demons

The Blood of Solomon

A Friend in Need

The Immortal Apprentice Trilogy

The War With Audin (Prequel Novella)

The Hunt For Revenge

The Army of Darkness

The Apprentice Reborn

The Soul Bound Saga

An Unwelcome Journey

Darkness in Tiber

Depths of Betrayal

The Black Iron Empire

Overmage

The Divine Key Trilogy

Shadow Magic

For The Greater Good

The Divine Key Awakens

The Portal Wars Saga

The Hidden Tower

Chains of the Fallen Omnibus

The Complete Soul Force Saga Omnibus

The Aegis of Merlin:

The Impossible Wizard

The Awakening

The Chimera Jar

The Raven's Shadow

Escape From the Dragon Czar

Wrath of the Dragon Czar

The Four Nations Tournament

Death Incarnate

Atlantis Rising

Rise of the Demon Lords

The Pale Princess

Malice

Aegis of Merlin Omnibus Vol 1.

Aegis of Merlin Omnibus Vol 2.

The Complete Aegis of Merlin Omnibus

Other Fantasy Novels:

The Squire

Death and Honor Omnibus

The Rogue Star Series:

Children of Darkness

Children of the Void

Children of Junk

Rogue Star Omnibus Vol. 1

Children of the Black Ship

Children of The End

ABOUT THE AUTHOR

James E. Wisher is a writer of science fiction and Fantasy novels. He's been writing since high school and reading everything he could get his hands on for as long as he can remember.

www.ingramcontent.com/pod-product-compliance
Lightning Source LLC
Chambersburg PA
CBHW050729250626
47155CB00005B/1724